Paradise

of the

Downcasts

Paradise of the Downcasts

A Collection of Short Tales & Essays

by

Nasreen Pejvack

Copyright © 2018 Nasreen Pejvack

Author: Nasreen Pejvack

Cover Design: Daniel Fanaei

                      Nasreen Pejvack

Website: http://examine-consider-act.ca

                      info@examine-consider-act.ca

ISBN: 978-1-7753223-0-6 (Paperback)

ISBN: 978-1-7753223-2-0 (eBook)

Paradise of the Downcasts: a collection of short stories / by Nasreen Pejvack

McNally Robinson Booksellers

1120 Grant Avenue, Winnipeg, MB Canada R3M 2A6 Toll Free 1-800-561-1833

http://www.mcnallyrobinson.com/home

Paperback available at McNally Robinson Booksellers, and online

To the ones who share

humanity's home

with all

TABLE OF CONTENTS

Author Forward 8

Mediterranean Sea: A New Beginning 10

Her Story 42

The Dove of Peace...52

Zermatt Will Always Be a Dream 59

Where Is My Food? 63

Let Me Love You..69

Racism 116

A Dog's Life in Iran versus the West....................... 123

Paradise of the Downcasts 129

Alsoomse 160

Tiny 174

Refugees 195

WILL 199

My Summer Vacation 201

Racism? Sexism? or Simply Lack of Accountability? 207

People 232

Acknowledgment 275

Author Biography 276

Author Forward

If I believe my Country is the planet Earth, then my loyalties lie there. I was born in the Middle-Eastern region, in the large province of Iran, in the city of Tehran. Throughout much of my adulthood, I have been on the north side of my country in the province of Canada, living in Ottawa and Vancouver. I have also lived in other provinces of this blue/green country, such as Greece and America, and in each I have learned much from its people and its culture.

In my childhood I thought that religion meant peace. I heard and read the representatives of each religion preach kindness and a better life for all. However, as I matured, I saw that they had lied. Religions killed many to convert others, or punished their own if they did not obey. So, my own religion developed into a simple love for humanity, and for this planet as my country, and for all life that accompanies us here.

This book is my life's learning and experiences in various parts of this beautiful Paradise, Canada. Let's work together in making it the best part of this precious planet, our home.

For over thirty years I have experienced all kinds of beautiful interactions with people of all walks of life. At the same time, I have heard of and seen injustices that I never expected to witness here in my beautiful Canada, a country that never really incited any international war. It's a country which has a social safety system better than most, yet one where countless people must turn to food banks regularly. Many have problems with paying for medications, and some die as a result. There are those who cannot attend or complete university because of inadequate support. And so here, the cruel cycles of poverty keep many excluded, just as in many other parts of our planet.

To ponder these problems, I present herein a series of independent short tales.

MEDITERRANEAN SEA: A NEW BEGINNING

Leaning on a rock, she sits on the shore of the blue Mediterranean Sea: a vast, endless, deep blue. She takes a deep breath and feels refreshed; even liberated. Be that as it may, it's nothing like the home she remembers. The air there had a very different scent to it. She closes her eyes to recall her father putting eucalyptus leaves into boiling water in the winter. The vapour smelled so invigorating. She misses him. She opens her eyes to look around and realizes how far away she is from her father, and everyone else she knew back home. It feels so strange. She takes in another deep breath and smiles. Her father always insisted that eucalyptus vapours were good, had health benefits, and helped prevent sickness in winter. Well, she doesn't know how true that statement is, but she has great nostalgia for that aroma.

A breeze caresses her face softly. She closes her eyes, takes another deep breath, and tries to relax and think of the family she left behind for good, and remember what was once there for her. She wonders why she does not seem to feel any regrets; perhaps it's because her family was so unsupportive.

She struggles to recall any pleasant or happy childhood memories, *"I left that house at such a young age. They weren't kind or accepting anyway, only judgmental and heartless. I don't miss the life they wanted for me. No, I do not want to remember them. My true family was my comrades; the ones I worked with. They became such an important part of my life. They filled my days so beautifully, and I miss them terribly. Yes, I miss them, and I will always cherish the sweet memories I had with every one of them."*

She sighs, looking out at the sea with tearful eyes, remembering how many were killed, imprisoned or, just like herself, had to flee because of their beliefs.

She considers that the best years of her life were in the company of those deeply dedicated people who cared very much about this world and its people. It saddens her that those dearest to her heart don't exist anymore.

Before she finishes her thoughts, she hears somebody speaking behind her. She turns and sees an older man talking to her. Unfortunately, it's only her second week in Athens so she does not speak or understand the language. She responds, "Sorry, no Greek."

He smiles and says, "Ah, English!"

"Yes, somewhat."

He sits beside her and asks if she is alone. She points to a boy playing on the beach, and reluctantly tells the man that she is here with her son.

"How long have you been here?"

"About two weeks."

"Oh, where from?"

"Iran." She hopes curt answers will make the man feel uncomfortable, and sure enough he kindly asks if he is bothering her. She says nothing, and continues staring out at the blue seascape. The man shifts awkwardly, but he is curious and stays seated.

She closes her eyes again and ignores the intruder, going back to her musings. However, the man breaks into her thoughts again by asking, "How was life back home?"

"Simple."

"Why did you leave?"

"Standing up for truth is dangerous there, and demanding one's human rights can be deadly."

He then a

sks the wrong question, "Where is your husband?" She stares at him for a long time, then says angrily, "You can leave now."

The man does not expect such a firm response, so he gets up to leave. She thinks, *"What a nosy man. It seems this culture is similar to my own. But for the language, I could think he is Iranian. Such an infuriating guy!"*

It is getting cool and dark, so she gets up and calls her boy. They hold hands and walk along the seaside toward their hotel in Glyfada. She is so worried about their future and where they should go since Greece is not an option. For now, she knows that she needs to find a job soon or their money will be gone.

The next day they go to the city centre. As they are walking along the busy streets they pass several clothing stores. She tells her son, "I can sew; maybe I should go in to ask where they produce these pretty dresses."

They enter one of the stores and she asks if anyone speaks English. A kind-looking lady comes close to say, "Hello, can I help you?"

Holding her son, she tells the lady that they are alone here and that she is looking for sewing work.

The lady regards her kindly and motions to follow her. She follows but is nervous. She finds herself gripping her son's hand tightly. Behind a pretty display wall, they walk down a hallway past some offices, and soon find themselves in a room at the back of the building where there are a few sewing machines and some women at work on them. The kind lady, who seems to be the owner, gives her an assortment of design-cut fabrics and asks if she can put them together. Never has she been so grateful for the long hours of labour she put in on the industrial garment machines at the factory back home where she had worked, while being an activist. She sits behind one of the machines and begins to sew a girl's dress. In short order she presents it to the lady, and before you know it she has a job.

It's June and now that she is employed, her next worry is to see if she can put her boy in some sort of school or summer activities for the time being. She soon learns that she cannot put her son in a Greek school, so she enrols him in an English summer school. They move out of the hotel into a small apartment in the city centre near her work. She is hoping that she and her son just have to keep busy for now, until a counter-revolution in Iran allows them to return home. But it becomes clear that Iran's government is still killing at will and that nothing is getting better there, only worse.

She also sees that she will have to leave beautiful Greece, as government policy there does not accept immigrants. She can have no status unless she marries a Greek man. Given her mindset and what happened right before she left Iran, such a thing is totally out of the question, even though her boss' son has already unsuccessfully asked her out several times.

She thinks about going to Switzerland, but any time she brings it up, her son disagrees, saying, "I do not want to learn French or German - why there?"

She cannot explain it to him, and so she simply drowns in her thoughts: *"I want to go there to see where he lived, breathed, walked and talked. I want to roam the forests he explored, climb the mountains he enjoyed; perhaps I can feel him in the air of that land, or possibly find his family."* At such times she often becomes breathless and agitated, and just stops debating about where to go next, leaving the matter be.

Every day after school, her boy meets her at work and waits for her shift to finish, then they go shopping or walking before returning home. One day, as they are taking a new route home, she hears a flapping sound above. Looking up she sees a beautiful white and red flag with a red maple leaf in the middle. She and her boy both like it for not having a sword or a gun or stars on it. It doesn't seem to be expressing aggression or supremacy; it just sports a pretty maple leaf. They smile at each other then walk through the doors of the Canadian embassy.

The photos on the walls are wonderfully inviting, with scenes of different parts of Canada artfully displayed all around the building. The two young attendants are friendly and informative, answering all their questions. She and her boy leave the embassy knowing that Canada is the place they want to go. The very next day she begins the process of securing their resettlement to Canada.

Within six months they are in Canada, settled in the city of Ottawa. For the first few months she is busy finding a place for them to live, getting her son into school, and then researching what she wants to do and what kind of skills she will need to begin her new life.

During that busy time, she keeps an eye out for people who may look like the native peoples of this land that she learned about in her birthplace, but she doesn't know if they will be speaking different languages or how they might look; darker skin perhaps, or beautiful long black hair? She isn't sure. One day she goes to school a bit early to pick up her son and waits by the door to see if any Indigenous people come to pick up their own children. She sees none - neither parents nor students.

She begins to wonder why she cannot see them anywhere, even wondering whether any had survived the wars of conquest she had heard and read about. She wants to ask people, though she does not know how. To her mind, the Indigenous people were the first people of this huge continent and they should be everywhere. As a new arrival to her new home, she sees there are many things that she knows nothing about it. She needs time to learn.

For now, her first priority is to concentrate on choosing a field of study that will help secure a job to support her little family of two. She selects the computer field because the college counsellor guarantees that, since high-tech companies are booming, she will learn skills that are in high demand. So, she begins a computer science program, all the while looking around, reading and asking questions to get to know her new home better.

Over the course of her first term, she manages to make some close friends. One is a sweet girl and they spend much of their time studying together. Her father's family was from Portugal while her mother's was from England, though both parents were born in Canada. One day at their lunch break, she boldly brings up the subject of Indigenous people, asking what happened to the first people of this land before her parents or other Europeans arrived. Where are they? Why do I not see them around like everybody else?

"Oh," her friend says, regarding her for a bit. "Good question. I think they are mostly living on reserves."

"What is a reserve?"

"A place that is their land and they live there together."

"And where is that?"

"I don't know, at the edges of cities I guess," her friend says.

Well, that is not good enough for her. She wants to know why people that she heard had lived here for thousands of years were not easily seen on the streets, at workplaces, and in schools, like everybody else. Also, she learns that, though her friend is a very nice person, she doesn't know much about First Nations people, and doesn't seem to care to know. It is disappointing.

She begins to search, gradually learning what reserves are and where they are located. She hears about one between Ottawa and Oshawa and finds out exactly where it is. She buys a map, then one morning, after dropping her son off at school, she goes to uncover a most heartbreaking situation in her beloved Canada.

After a pleasant drive of a couple of hours, she arrives at what they call a reserve. She is shocked! She feels like she has left Canada and entered into a third world country. The area is run down, with houses so old that it's a very different scene than what she sees in Ottawa, or in any other nice small town she encountered on the way.

She notices a corner store and goes in, but doesn't see much on the shelves – nothing of any good quality. She looks around feeling dizzy, needing to lean against the wall. The shopkeeper sees this visitor looking rather unwell and hurries over to her, holding her hand and helping her to a chair. Without asking, the shopkeeper runs to the back of the store to bring her some water, but before drinking it she notices the water is beige; not as clear as water should be. She looks at the shopkeeper with suspicion, wondering if she is trying to poison her. The shopkeeper notices, takes the water away, and brings some bottled water. The visitor takes the water with appreciation and smiles at the shopkeeper.

Leaning back on the chair, she has a sip of water, asking, "Is this a ghost town?"

"No, there's a community living here. This is a reserve, did you know?"

"Yes, but why is it so run down? It's nothing like Ottawa, where I live. Why?"

"Simple. We are not accepted; haven't you read or heard of our stories?"

"No, I cannot see people like you where I live, which is why I am here. I thought there is nothing left of you people."

The shopkeeper laughs aloud and gives her a friendly pat on the back.

"Really? You sweet girl! You should know there were many tribes on this continent, but after Europeans came here and took everything, they began to change us and our way of living. Now, they want us to live as they see fit. Who are you by the way, and why do you want to know? Are you a reporter from another country?"

"Um, no. I'm a newcomer, living in Ottawa for a little over a year. I asked friends and neighbours where the first people of this continent are, but they didn't seem to know, nor did they seem to like my questioning. So, I found out more about you guys myself, and here I am. Why you are in a reserve?"

The shopkeeper looks at her for a few seconds with a kind smile, "You live in Ottawa and drove here just to see what a reserve is, and where my people are?"

"Yes, there's nothing wrong with that; I like to know," she says in a firm voice.

"Hmm, you are a different kind. You did not see any of us in Ottawa?"

"No, I did not. I have seen movies and read books about your way of life. But when I came to Canada and didn't see any of you in school or the workplace or on the street, I thought the Europeans had destroyed all the first peoples of this land. That saddened me deeply. I had to know."

She looks into the shopkeeper's face, trying to read her emotions. The shopkeeper looks at her intensely, not knowing what to make of this curious stranger.

"Well, they almost destroyed us, and those of us left are emotionally hurt, and many are not stable. However, there are actually some who work in the cities and in businesses; well-educated ones. Perhaps you don't see them because there are just a few of us compared to the large number of Europeans. Some did their best and have a good education with well-paying jobs, but the majority are forgotten and living in poor conditions."

The shopkeeper sighs and looks at this young woman who came all the way from Ottawa on a mission. In silence they exchange a tense but affectionate look.

The traveller takes another sip of her water, then asks, "How much for the water?"

"For you, nothing," says the shopkeeper.

"No, I insist! This is your shop and this water came from that fridge, meaning it's for sale. Please let me know how much." She is uncomfortable, feeling distressed that the shopkeeper does not want to charge her.

Sensing her discomfort, the shopkeeper puts her hand on this stranger's shoulder, and with a kind smile says, "Please don't be upset. I will charge you next time. Then maybe you'll come back. I'll tell you about our tap water then, and why it's so bad, and many other stories. Will you come again?"

"Oh, I will, I will! I would love to hear you. I want to know all the whys."

They talk some more, then they set a date and time for next month. She leaves the little run-down town, still in disbelief. All the way back she thinks about the paradise she thought she had come to, comparing the pros and cons, the good and evil in all the various parts of this world, and contrasting that to Canada, her little haven. She whispers, *"If they were smart enough to stay away from most belligerent wars, that should mean there are many ethical humanists here. So why don't they correct this mistake?"* She gets home exhausted, not because of the long drive - that was absolutely beautiful - but because of what she had learned of her new home.

Busy with her daily life, the month passes by in a hurry. Soon it's time to return to the First Nation town. She takes a box of pastry from the fridge leaving her home feeling apprehensive. She drops her son off at school and then is on her way, wending once more through the beautiful scenery. She reflects on how the farms and woods and lakes along all the Canadian roads seemed so fresh and natural. *"Perhaps,"* she thinks, *"it's because there weren't many battles of greed raging over the terrain among the people who lived here before the Europeans arrived. They were in harmony with nature and did not harm the land."*

She continues driving, enjoying her surroundings, and eventually arrives at the sullen little town. She goes directly to the store, and to her surprise there is a bit of a crowd there talking and laughing, boisterous and cheerful.

As soon as she enters, they all turn to her with welcoming smiles and gather around her one by one to say hello, giving her hugs, or shaking her hand. She smiles timidly and returns their greetings, then someone pats her on the shoulder and says, "So, you want to know how we ended up here, hey?" She smiles and only nods.

They offer her a chair and she puts the box of pastry on the table as everyone gathers around. The storekeeper has been standing in a corner watching things with a warm smile. She joins the others and sits right across from her.

"It was so nice of you to come again. I talked about our last meeting to the elders of our town, they talked to a few others, and one thing led to another and now we have a crowd here to see who this curious young woman is searching us out. I know it's a bit overwhelming for you; sorry about that. But look at the bright side; you will have many stories, from many different points of view, and definitely from different experiences. What do you say?

And what are these delicious looking pastries! We've never had these before!"

"There are a few Iranian shops in Montreal. My son and I drive there some Sundays to buy our favourites. We went there yesterday, so I thought I would buy something for today." She pushes the box to the middle of the table saying cheerfully, "Please help yourselves!"

Everyone tries the sweets and compliments the interesting varieties and the wonderful taste. They talk about the diversity of cultures all across the globe, and she happily engages with them and answers their questions. They ask about her son, her job, her studies, and even her age. When they find out she has no family in Canada but her son, they look at her sadly, especially when they learn she can never go back to her birthplace.

A young woman says, "Ah, I don't think I could live without my mother. I feel so sad and sorry for you."

Another lady says, "I understand how you feel as I had to live without my mother. Not because I left her, but because they took me away from her by force and sent me to residential school."

The lady has tears in her eyes and there is an awkward moment of silence. The visitor breaks it by asking, "What is residential school?"

They all look intently at her, then begin to tell their stories about those institutions and how they were administered by churches and backed by governments that had no understanding or acceptance of Indigenous cultures or ways of life. One by one the people around the table talk about how the schools tried to change and educate Indigenous children into a European way of life and how damaging and hurtful the whole system was.

They tell her that the residential school system operated from the 1840s right through to today, that they have fought hard to close those schools, yet there are still a few operating in some areas. Various emotions rise around the table, some anger, some sadness, but everyone is quiet as each person speaks. They talk about how the system forcibly separated children from their families for extended periods of time and prevented them from acknowledging their heritage and culture or from speaking their own languages. They talk about how they were severely punished if they did not obey the strict rules, and speak of horrendous abuses at the hands of school staff; physical, sexual, emotional, and psychological. They speak of how devastating the consequences were, and how they still suffer from them to this day.

"Hey, hey," says a woman from across the room, and everyone turns to her. She looks particularly gloomy as she glares back at them all, and with a bitter smile asks this young visitor, "Have you heard about Residential School Syndrome?"

"No, I am sorry; and what does that mean?"

"They took more than 150,000 children from their families, forcing them to live in strange new conditions where they experienced traumatic abuses and were made to feel ashamed of who they were. The children felt abandoned, not understanding why they were in those schools or why their parents did not defend them and take them back home. They felt alone and isolated, not realizing that their parents were victims too and had no power over their circumstances. These youngsters had to deal with all these feelings alone at such a young age, and the emotional difficulties manifested as depression, anxiety, then rage and anger, and thereafter addiction, suicide and other mental illnesses. All together these symptoms are called Residential School Syndrome."

The young visitor sits there alarmed and angry, staring at them with tearful eyes. She then whispers, "What a cruelty. Why did they think they were entitled to do what they did?" Raising her voice, she says angrily, "You know, you are not the only ones to have these painful experiences. Colonial powers moved around the world occupying lands and changing cultures at will. What happened to you happens all around our world.

Moreover, I am sure you all know how they captured and brought Africans over to Europe and the Americas for slavery, and how brutal life was in those days. Ha! And do you think things are different at this time? Well these days their tactics and strategies have changed, and now a rich mix of international corporations backed by their Chinese, Russian, American, and the same old European governments, are controlling and exploiting nations worldwide. And they have organized things so well that we are all helping them in their agenda without our knowing."

The storekeeper looks at her with a big smile, winks, and says, "Is that so, and how are we helping them?"

"Well, banks, financial institutions, big oil, and other multinational giants are controlling the world's assets, and we often work for them, even competing with each other for the good jobs they provide as we strive to attain a rich and comfortable lifestyle advertised daily by the corporate media. We have to work and provide for our families, so indirectly we are supporting these monsters. They are using us, and because of a lack of awareness, we are willingly helping them become wealthier, while at the same time many communities like yours all across the world are impoverished. Corporate interests control natural resources for which they install and topple governments, and all the while you and I, in these supposedly democratic lands, battle for some of the spoils."

A young man says, "We are not competing with anyone; we don't believe in their way of life."

The visitor looks at him, and takes a deep breath, "Well, just by buying things you are often supporting that system, but I hear you. It sounds like your main concern here is to make sure you fight for your children, and don't allow them to be taken."

"Oh, there are not many more residential schools; we have fought to eliminate them and soon they'll all be closed," he says with a satisfied smile. "But the wounds are still there."

A young woman says, "Yes, the residential schools are closing down, but my sister's kid is still living with a white family and my husband and I cannot adopt her."

The visitor turns to her and says, "What do you mean by that?"

The young lady says, "I mean, if something goes wrong with one of the families on the reserve and there is a child involved, we cannot adopt that child. Family services gives the child to whomever they think is right, and from their point of view th

at's usually a white family."

People around the table now begin to discuss that phenomenon with each other as if they had just sunny afternoon , enjoying remembered this new problem in their town. They forget all about their guest as they report to one another what each of them are doing and at what stage they are in their efforts to change that law so as to allow them to keep their children if there is trouble in a family within their community.

She sits in her chair and listens intently to all the conversations, and thinks, *"Wow, and I thought I was living in paradise after escaping my own troubled land, but these people are not doing too well."* She sighs and listens some more, then notices the storekeeper gazing kindly at her.

They exchange a smile and the visitor gets up and goes to her host who hugs her and says, "Well, they are angry and a bit loud; would you like to come again, or are you satisfied with what you heard and learned today."

"Far from it, I only have more questions. It's okay to come again?"

"Sure, and I promise next time it will be only the two of us and I will answer your questions to the best of my knowledge and experience."

They hug once more, then the visitor says her goodbyes to everyone, thanking them for their patience with her.

She leaves and gets in her car, thinking about what she has heard, *"Not much difference really. People all over the world are hurt and exploited by whomever can get away with operating an unjust system."* She drives away with a different perspective of her new country.

The next day she goes back to college and talks with her history teacher regarding her recent experience. Her teacher listens, smiling. "Those events happened a long time ago. You didn't need to go there to find out about them. They are fine now."

She is surprised to hear that from a history teacher. "Fine? Define fine, please. You are a history teacher and you don't even want to talk about them, or understand what really happened to the first peoples of this land!"

"Well, it really is a sad story, and many do not like to talk about it. But it's over now and we cannot do anything about the past. So tell me, what did you learn by going there?"

She pauses a bit, looking at him distrustfully, and then says, "I felt like I had entered a third world country as soon as I crossed into that reserve. I found that the people there were very nice and kind, wanting to help me to understand better. They wanted to know where I came from, whether I was living alone in Ottawa, and whether I can go and visit my family. They were so kind to me. I visited them a couple of times and they were quite accommodating. I am invited to go there again. It was great, and I learned a lot. As for you sir, do you know that it is 1989 and yet there are still some residential schools operating here and there?"

Her teacher looks at her long and thoughtfully, "Good for you! I was born here and have lived here all my life, yet I don't often give much thought about the First Nations, nor cared to know how they are living. I feel rather ashamed and embarrassed."

"You should be embarrassed, and ashamed. You are the history teacher; why don't you research and find out for yourself? Perhaps after your research you will have real historical knowledge to teach. Then you can let your students know about what happened here. You will learn that the awful events that happened in the past, as you put it, are not yet corrected. What would you do about that?" She folds her arms and continues, "Perhaps that's why it has taken so long to correct the consequences of the past, and why residential schools have been at work for so long; why the native people of this land still live in such poor conditions. Maybe it's because you guys don't care to know about or correct the injuries that have been inflicted."

She pauses, thinking perhaps she should go now. But she has so much on her mind that she continues, "I have learned through my own reading that before Europeans came to this continent there were thousands of different tribes and tens of millions of Indigenous people living here. Today they are a little over a million here in Canada, and per capita even fewer in America. Now, considering how in countries around the world there have only been increases in population, the fact that the population of these people has shrunk greatly would suggest that there has been a genocide." She glares at him and then leaves the classroom, while he stands and reflects as she disappears around the corner.

She leaves the school to take a walk in the nearby woods, thinking of home where, as a teenager and later as a young adult, she had read books and seen movies depicting the lives of the people on the great North American landmass. In Greece, as beautiful as it was, she always had an uncertain future ahead of her, knowing she could not stay there, no matter how much she loved its weather or culture. Her goal and hope had been to go someplace away from the violent old history of the world. To her, Canada had seemed like a fresh new country with, as far as she knew, no history of violence. She is amazed how, since she arrived here, everything she thought she knew has been shattered. She feels confused and frightened, worried that there is nowhere safe on this little chunk of rock....

She thinks, *"Among all the creatures of this planet, we are the ones who evolved to be intelligent enough to invent, create and grow, but a greedy and cruel part of us has grown with us as well."*

She goes on with her life, reading and learning more about humanity's little home in this vast universe, but she grows more despondent, watching the many regrettable conducts of the world's supposedly intelligent species. She pities the ones who care for nothing but how to get richer and gain more power, with no regard for anything else but the self.

HER STORY

Charlotte sits at her apartment window, looking outside while thinking about her exams. The semester is over, though she is not happy. Not that she did badly; no, the exams all went as well as could be expected. She is worrying more about her next term and how she will manage the tuition and her other expenses with her meagre income.

Birds are chirping, soaring and dancing around within the branches of a huge willow tree outside her window. She smiles as she realizes that the cheerful activity means the rain has ended. Puffy white clouds are emerging, which also means the sun will be out soon, perhaps instilling a new energy into her day.

She is thinking of seeing the faculty's adviser to explain her situation and perhaps ask for more scholarship funds, but then she becomes distracted by the sky and starts to make stories with the clouds before they disappear. There's one, that big one, which looks like a whale; there are a few smaller ones around it that look just the same. She whispers, "Hmmm that looks like a mother whale and her children; it seems as if they are following her."

Suddenly there's a lump in her throat as she remembers her mother and how she suffered before leaving her and her brother all alone in this unkind world. She misses her. Getting up, she goes to her mother's picture on the wall to confirm once more that she really was the most beautiful woman she has ever known. She puts her finger on her lips and blows her a kiss...

She calls the university to make an appointment with the student adviser, then gets ready to go to work. She has a part-time job during the term which becomes full time between terms. No mystery as to why she's always tired and looks so pale.

After completing her shift for the day, she gets to her appointment with time to spare. She is reviewing what she needs to say when she hears her name: "Charlotte, you can come in now."

After a short question and answer, Charlotte asks, "Why do you guys change all the time? I would like to talk to Nancy; she knows everything about me. Where is she?"

The adviser smiles kindly, "Nancy is not here anymore my dear. My name is Kate, and I hope I can help you. Everything should be in the computer." Then she sits back to look at her, and continues, "You are in your third year. You have been a very good student with a very high GPA, but since last year your marks have been going down and you are not doing as well. May I ask why?"

"I have to work! I take care of myself as well as my brother who is in grade ten. Don't ask about my parents; there are none. My student loan is not enough for the two of us, and welfare does not help because they want me to work, which would mean dropping out of school, which would mean being poor forever; but I will not quit! So I am both working and attending school, but most of the time I am so tired that I barely have the energy to study. And we can't get enough nutritious food, so when I do study, I keep forgetting the material. My brother even works part time, but it's still not enough. I work, I don't have time to study and I'm not eating properly; that's why my marks are going down."

Kate looks at her for some time, and then says, "I still would like to know about your parents."

Charlotte looks agitated and angry, but she knows she has to answer. "My father passed away in a car accident when I was ten. My mother passed last year; she suffered after a long agonizing battle with a devastating sickness, that wiped out all her life savings because medications were very expensive and she had no insurance. We thought medical care was free in our supposedly advanced country, until my mother became ill. Since last year, I have been taking care of my brother and myself. The student loan is not covering all our expenses, and our part-time jobs don't pay enough to cover rent, utilities, food and above all the expensive tuition and books. To be honest, I am already up to my eyeballs in student loan debt, but I can't see keeping this up without taking on even more. Every day after I leave school, I go to work, most of the time until midnight. So lack of sleep has affected my health, my emotions, my attention span, and of course my memory; with the end result that my academic work is suffering.

"You know, it's so ironic. For my sociology class I wrote an essay about poverty and education. In my research, I learned that the UN designated October 17th as the International Day for the Eradication of Poverty. That was in 1993, and now more than two decades have passed, we all seem to be struggling just the same, if not worse."

Kate looks impressed, "You are very smart. So how was your mark on that assignment?" Charlotte responds that she hasn't received the mark yet, but that at this point her only concern is whether or not the school can help her.

Kate examines Charlotte's file, looking for a way to help her. But she already has a scholarship, and with her marks going down, the calculations just don't add up for her to qualify for more assistance.

Charlotte watches Kate clicking away intently at the computer, anxiously hoping for a satisfying answer. She feels trapped in a cycle of poverty. She remembers those times after her dad died and her mom had to provide for the three of them, and they would go to sleep hungry. Nevertheless, Mom always made sure that Charlotte studied well and went to classes, helping her enter university with some of the highest marks of her senior year class. Yet here she was now at a crossroads where she may not be able to complete her studies.

Charlotte feels that a long time has passed. She tries to be patient as she occupies herself with looking around the office. From time to time she looks back at Kate, trying to read her face. She thinks about the latest assignment she just handed in, wherein she learned that in a recent UNICEF survey, Canada ranked below average for child poverty in relation to other rich nations. She smiles cynically and thinks about how, even though she is not a child anymore, she and her brother nevertheless were in that category, all because a broken system failed to protect them. She thinks, *"The circle of poverty will make sure people like us fail because no access to higher education results in the lack of a well-paying job, which then dooms my children to live in the same circumstances, and onward it goes…"*

Kate stops her sad train of thought by saying, "I am so sorry Charlotte, but you are not eligible. I tried everything I could to see if I can enrol you in some kind of compensation, but the result is negative."

Charlotte feels cold. She also looks pale, which worries Kate who gets up to approach her, saying, "I want you to know that I too believe our system has not been set up properly, and it is not fair to many. I wish we were like the Scandinavian countries where universities are free, where the young there don't have to face what you are facing here. But this is our system and I don't know what to say. Look, how about you work a few more hours and take fewer courses? You may graduate a bit later but eventually you will."

Charlotte won't hear her anymore. She rises from her chair, gives Kate a chilly look, and leaves her office.

Kate runs after her to out, "I will try more and I'll call you." Charlotte doesn't respond. She leaves the school and walks toward her apartment, remembering that they have not had a good nutritious meal for a couple of nights now and the fridge is empty. It kills her to think she may have to go to a food bank.

As she walks into her home she angrily whispers, "I was a gifted student throughout my elementary and secondary years, and I entered university with a good scholarship. Now here I am falling behind because I'm hungry, tired, sleepy and constantly worried about my brother. Was I not a good child of this country? I do not want to go to a food bank; nobody should be forced into such a situation."

"Who are you talking to? Are you okay?" her brother asks anxiously.

"Ah, sorry. I didn't notice you are home."

"Sure, I've been home for a while now, but why are you talking to yourself? You look so upset."

Charlotte holds his hand and guides him to a chair in their tiny kitchen. She sits across the table still holding his hand and looks at him lovingly and kindly, then softly says, "I am not getting any more money from my school, at least not for this term, so I'm going to have to drop two of my courses so that I'll have more time to work more hours."

"No, you are already in university; I can pick up more hours!"

"No! No," Charlotte says angrily, "You are to graduate from your high school young man! Concentrate on getting good marks for me, and never, ever say such a thing again. We will manage. I am sure it will only be for this term; next term I will be full time again. I promise you, no matter how long it takes, I will not quit."

He has tears in his eyes as they grip each other's hands, and he cries, "I miss mom...."

"I miss her too..."

Then they get up and go to the window hand-in-hand, where they hold each other to look up at the clouds into an unknown future.

THE DOVE OF PEACE

It relaxes me to go for a walk when I am under stress, in particular when I have a difficult task ahead of me, such as the essay I had been asked to write concerning the status of peace in the world today. So, I took a walk on a sunny afternoon, sunny afternoon, enjoying the magnificent view and listening to the distant, endless, musical sound of a waterfall. I sat in a comfortable spot, and as I invented stories using the magical shapes of clouds drifting silently overhead, I heard close by the flapping wings of a bird, then sudden quiet. I looked around to see a striking white dove sitting on a branch, enjoying the same marvellous view. I thought, *"Oh, aren't you a fine-looking dove. You know, they say you are the symbol of peace."*

I remembered when I was a young student, and I had to write an essay about peace; about how the world was a safer place than in the days of the cave-dwellers. Now here I was again, not as young as I used to be, faced with the same assignment. Two literature teachers from two completely different cultures, thousands of miles apart, both asked me to write about peace and our awe-inspiring human rights. What an intriguing experience!

I took small pieces of my bread and threw them out for the dove. The bird wouldn't move at first, but then finally flew down and started to eat the crumbs. As I enjoyed watching the bird, I remembered the trouble I had with that first assignment years before. I couldn't agree with the professor that the world was a safer place and that we had more peace today.

Writing had always been an easy task for me, yet I wasn't able to begin that assignment; not because I didn't know how to start or because I didn't believe in human advancement, but because I believed that this very advancement was, in many ways, working against peace.

The professor talked about how technology had brought us from living in caves to the stunning architecture of our modern cities. I argued then. Now I was arguing again. Yes, we have modern cities, but we also have modern weapons to destroy those cities... and how intelligent is that? We have sciences that describe DNA, and to some extent understand human psychology, but we also have technologies that can destroy both with chemical weapons. Our activists talk about and fight for human rights, peace, and a clean environment for our future generations, but there is no true peace yet, and toxins are still being released into nature.

I gave a bit more bread to the bird, remembering that I eventually did write that assignment and called it, "The Dove of Peace." The starting point was when Noah created his ark and wanted to run away from the world's madness and save humankind and many other species.

When the rains that flooded the earth stopped pouring down, Noah sent out various birds to see if they would bring back any sign of land to his boat. He was anxious to begin life again on solid ground. One dove eventually returned carrying an olive branch in her beak. That white dove became the symbol of peace on earth. I moved closer to the bird, slowly approached it, and with one quick motion picked it up.

The bird was shocked, but as I started stroking it gently and offering it bread, the bird relaxed and ate from my hand. As I patted the bird, I thought about how, some thousands of years after Noah, there were a few Persian warriors who became tired of fighting over lands and religions. They ran into the mountains to start a new peaceful life with their people. I spoke to the dove, "They used you, beautiful bird, as a messenger of peace. I am sure many other nations used you symbolically in their folk stories about peace. Yet ancient wars continued, so that we eventually experienced our modern deadly World Wars.

"After World War II, Pablo Picasso was responsible for an influential use of the dove of peace. He designed and illustrated a unique-looking dove, just like you, for the international peace congress in Paris in 1949."

I sadly stroked the bird thinking about how that congress had not brought about the end of conflict. We subsequently had many wars, each of which aimed to bring peace – how hypocritical! "Many of your kind were released in celebration any time a war was over, but there was always another war. Since the time of the Epic of Gilgamesh, graphic artists such as Picasso, have produced an endless series of doves-of-peace in different shapes, but human societies could never actually bring tranquility to this world."

As I gently held my bird, I thought about a 3-D play-card image I had seen of an American bomber that alternated between a dove and a hawk. I thought about government propaganda posters from Turkey and China that make free use of the dove of peace as easily as those same governments make free use of violence to achieve their ends. I recalled the image of the dove squatting peacefully on a Palestinian scarf or hidden in the hands of militant youngsters from Eastern Europe.

I put the bird down to whisper, "Hey lovely bird, it seems you belong to conflicts of all kinds and you don't even know it. Peace is just one of many words in the dictionary. You are a counterfeit, manufactured, ineffective symbol." I let the dove fly away free, taking with it my hope for peace in this world.

What does it mean that after ten odd years I was facing the same challenge of describing a peace that still didn't exist? With courage gained from my stunning encounter with the dove, I went back to my professor with only two options. Either I write about peace in the only place it can be found – the narrow, false one in my small suburban neighbourhood – or I write of what I really think about the state of human rights and peace in the

world. Option two, he said, but don't be too graphic.

ZERMATT WILL ALWAYS

BE A DREAM

The scenery is breathtaking, and I feel as if I am dreaming. What a sight I see before me as I sit on a cliff looking down over the valley. The Matterhorn faces me. To my right a stretch of the Alps holds the shorter green foothills against its chest, creating a stunning view. To the left is a set of spectacular cliffs; they're flat and green on top with a river running off the edge, cascading down as a magnificent waterfall rushing down to the valley below, forming another river winding along the valley and through a picturesque town. The colourful rooftops of the houses add so much to this beauty.

I hear a kind, warm voice behind me. "We will sit here a bit longer. The sun is going down, and you really must see the mountains at sunset. It is like the most amazing, intriguing painting you have ever seen, except it's real. It is Mother Nature!"

Happily, I smile at him, asking where he has been. "Right here, looking at you. You were enjoying the view so much, and I loved seeing that. I have missed you."

I look into his kind eyes to ask, "Where are we?"

"Matter valley, and under your feet is the town of Zermatt. You know the Matterhorn, don't you?"

"Yes I do, and there it is! Are we in Switzerland?" I ask sheepishly. "Did I sleep all the way here?"

He does not say a word; he just looks at me and then holds me so tight that I can barely breathe. He whispers, "In just a few more minutes it will be darker, people will turn on their house lights, and the view of the valley will become a sparkling array of colourful lights. You will love it!"

I relax patiently in his arms, and together we wait for nightfall. As we are appreciating the view, he whispers softly, "Why do you never let me hold you like this?"

I turn to him, looking into his loving hazel eyes once more. "I am sorry, I didn't know better." Then I hear an alarm clock ringing. I look at him again.

With teary eyes he says, "Don't go, don't go…"

I feel a gentle touch on my face, "Wake up sleepyhead, didn't you hear the alarm? We're going to miss our flight!" Then a kiss on my cheek, and I open my eyes to see beautiful blue eyes and a kind smile. I look quickly around, frightened and confused. Am I not in Switzerland? Where am I, if not with him?

Ah, no, I'm in a hotel in Canada with my husband on our holiday.

He holds me tight, "Hmm, I'm so sorry. You were dreaming again. I hope it wasn't too bad." He kisses my head.

I feel like I'm losing it, as tears begin running down my face. I have nothing to say to my love. Here we are on vacation together, yet I am a world away.

"It's okay, you'll soon feel better. Would you like a cup of tea?"

"No, thank you. Do we have time for a shower? I would like to take a shower."

"Sure, you go do that, and I will pack."

I cannot even look into his kind face. He knows I was dreaming of my past life. When was it, thirty-four years ago? He knows there were many sad stories which are still haunting me. But courageously and kindly he stands right beside me with love and compassion, with the promise that he is always there for me.

WHERE IS MY FOOD?

The sun peeks in through a little hole in her small, dark, cold room. The smell of dirt and mould fills the air. She is tired and hungry, stretching her weak body and yawning. Her twin toddlers are all over her and searching for her breasts. They suckle contently, all the while playfully shoving each other. They break away to wrestle some more, then return to their mother, even though they get nothing from those empty breasts hanging on her body.

She plays with them gently, holding her young against her tired body, kissing them. She slowly gets up to look around the empty space, knowing they need food. She goes to the entrance and pokes her head outside. It feels warm, with a fresh smell of spring in the air. She very much enjoys the feel of the sun on her face.

She steps outside and the two little ones follow. She looks around and sees the same two paths, and she remembers. If she goes to the left, she will come to a graveyard of tree stumps, and then that mean city with those wild and selfish beasts in their fancy homes ... the ones who attacked her for who she is. She had to run away from them last year, so she takes the right-hand path, a way that winds through more pleasant and forested land.

Her body is weak so that she wobbles a bit as she walks. The two little ones seem fine for now; perky and playful as they happily follow her. So far, their tummies are full. She has no milk anymore but she lets her kids suckle any time they want. Soon she is deep in the familiar forest and begins searching for berries, or anything else she can find, to feed her children and fill her own empty belly. After searching for a couple of hours, all they find are a few little wild berries. She arrives at the river where she used to catch fish, but the water is so low that there is no way any fish could live there. She is hungry and breathless, and now her kids are hungry and impatient. She is getting worried. Then she hears the familiar humming and buzzing sounds of the beasts. Frightened, she pushes her children behind her to make them understand that they must not get ahead of her and only follow behind.

They walk a bit more, arriving at the edge of another town. They see many dens, each one with large smelly bins where she may be able to find food. She gets her kids to hide and stay quiet, then she sits with them and waits for dark. They are all hungry. She hates those bins as she knows the food in there is like poison in their stomach, but she also knows it's better than nothing. She sits leaning against a big tree as her kids suckle on her empty breasts. She cuddles with them and looks at them proudly, seeing how brimful of life they are despite their hunger.

Eventually she feels it is dark enough, though they still must be quiet. She remembers well from the year before on the other side of the forest how the monsters there suddenly arrived with loud noises and colourful flashing eyes, and how she barely escaped by running back into the woods.

Her kids sense that they must not make noise while following their mother, as she stealthily approaches one of the smaller bins then tries to open it. She works away and eventually opens it to drag out a few plastic bags which she carries quickly back to the forest. They are so hungry as they rip apart the foul-smelling bags. They eat whatever is edible.

Walking slowly into the forest after their meal, they climb a tree. She pulls her kids to her chest so they can relax and get some rest after their adventurous day. The twins are uncomfortable and restless because of the unsavoury food they ate, but they manage to sleep through the night and some of the next morning. For the rest of the day they search around for berries, but any direction they go they encounter the mean beasts.

That evening, she desperately comes back to the same place as the previous night, waiting again for nightfall, and then approaching another garbage bin. However, before she can open it, lights suddenly flash in her eyes. Those monsters start shouting. Panicking, she runs back into the forest yelling for her kids. They follow her, but so do four of the monsters. She hears a loud bang and then feels a sudden pain in her body. She tries to keep running but she becomes very weak and soon collapses. Her kids jump onto her, and she tries to hide them against her hairy belly, but she has no energy. She tries to lick them, but suddenly they are lifted up. She looks frantically at them as they are carried away toward those colourful flashing eyes of the monsters, all the while screaming for her.

She tries to get up but she cannot; she has lost too much blood. She moans and looks in the direction that her children were taken away, trying desperately to see them, but she can only hear their cries. She lets out a gurgling roar, and it seems tears run down her face, as she weakly calls to them.

Two police officers stand over her head. The tall one says, "Why did you shoot her, you moron?"

"He came right up to the houses and into the garbage; we can't have that. Besides, I thought he was ready to attack me."

"He? Don't be so clueless! She is a mother bear; just a hungry mother bear trying to feed her cubs, just like we do!"

Her ears are up, still trying to hear her children's cries. She takes her last breath, as the moron says, "Is she crying? I didn't know bears cry too!"

LET ME LOVE YOU

The psychiatric ward is deafening, with patients restless and noncompliant. A nurse is picking up the food tray that Victor had tossed away while angrily screaming that he hates this food, and "how many times do I have to tell you." He is shouting and trashing anything at hand. Then he hears the security team arrive and begin to close the main doors.

Victor knows that when these guys come and close those doors, it means that the big restraining nurses will soon be there and he will probably be administered a tranquilizer. He puts his head down and quickly returns to his room, closes the door, and sits quietly.

After several minutes he gets up, opens the door just as quietly, and has a peek to see what is going on. Yes, the muscle-men are around sending everyone to their rooms, and the ward is getting quieter by the minute.

He goes back to his table, picks up his book and sits in front of the window. He tries to read, but is restless and angry as he tries to remember if he himself had started the commotion. After some time, there's a knock on the door and his doctor enters the room. "It seems you like it here and you don't want to leave; what do you say Victor?"

Victor looks sullenly at the floor, and after a brief silence looks up at his doctor and meekly asks, "Did I start the fight?"

"No, but you contributed greatly. I watched the video. You trashed your food tray, and the poor nurse was frightened. If you want to leave this hospital to live with your sister, you must know that there will always be things out there that you may not like. If all you can do is react violently, then you will just end up back here and it will be for a longer stay."

The doctor pauses, looking kindly at Victor. Then he sits down across the table, looks into Victor's eyes, and holds his hand gently. "I know you are a smart young man; a top student before your accident. This behaviour is the result of your head trauma. It will take time for you to improve and get back to your old life. The new meds are effective and you are faithfully doing your exercises, physically and emotionally. We only need you to co-operate and…"

But before he completes his sentence the door opens and Lilly enters the room, eager to see her brother again. With one look though, her warm smile quickly fades as she sees that something has happened.

Victor gets up and rushes to her. He holds her hand eagerly saying, "I didn't start the fight! There was so much noise and I just did not like that food!" Lilly holds him, caressing his hair. "You promised me to try harder, and to do your best to handle such things. You have to come home soon. Don't you want that my darling?"

"I'll let you two have a few minutes to talk. Lilly, please come and see me before you leave."

"Sure doctor, I'll be there."

She then sits with her brother, holds his hands, and asks what happened.

"I really don't know. I was in the common area, then suddenly everyone was shouting and making noises, my head began to hurt, and the nurse was right then trying to feed me that disgusting food." He pauses for a moment, then sadly says, "I lost it, didn't I?"

"Seems like it. I don't know any details just yet, but you know better Victor. I need you home. It's been over a year that you have been here. Your stitches have healed and you can read and write again. You are improving daily. Look, the doctor said as soon as you feel something is bothering you, you should remove yourself from the situation and get away. Why didn't you go outside for a walk in the garden? You said it helps."

"Yes, yes! I should have. I promise you, next time these crazy people begin to screech I will leave, come to my room, and close my door. Yes, and … and listen to music so I don't hear them. Yes … I will."

Lilly holds him again and kisses his head saying, "Can I take you to the cafeteria for some breakfast?"

"I would love that!"

"Okay, let me go to see the doctor while you wash your face and change."

Lilly leaves Victor's room and walks quickly toward the doctor's office. When she arrives he is talking with someone in the corridor. As soon as he sees her, he dismisses the gentleman and asks her to follow him to his room. He offers her a chair and Lilly sits, anxious for him to begin.

The doctor looks at her intently and asks, "How have you been?"

"I'm fine, thank you! How is he and what happened? Last week you told me he is much better."

"And he is much better; although he still has problems with noises and people. I cannot release him next week Lilly!"

"What? You said he is much better and that we can go home, then see you weekly!" says Lilly, agitated.

"I know, but then we had today's event. Actually, today I wanted to talk to you about a new idea. Please hear me out."

Lilly reluctantly settles into her chair respectfully asserting that she is listening.

After a short pause the doctor says, "Look, he listens to classical music a lot, and it seems to calm him. This is wonderful, because you do not see many young people today appreciate or understand this good music. So, I would like to ask a therapist friend of mine, who plays classical piano, to come and work with him."

"You mean a form of Art Therapy?"

"Yes, Victor had a traumatic brain injury – a concussion. Art Therapy has been known to help people recover from this kind of injury.

"This therapist used to be a great student of mine, and he is doing his PhD. It happens that he is about as good in his music as he is in his studies. I want to introduce you two to him, and if all goes well and Victor agrees to work with him, and of course if you like the idea, we could begin soon. So, shall we meet tonight?"

"But where are you planning to carry out this plan?"

"Ah! You know there is another wing off the north end of this facility, right across from the rose garden."

"Yes, Victor and I walk there sometimes. We have seen and admired that nice-looking building. We've peered through the windows and seen beautiful paintings on its walls. Yet we haven't seen anybody use the place. Maybe we were there at the wrong time. Yes, I think I know that building."

"Great. Well, it's called Garden House. That's where our Art Therapy section is. If all goes well tonight, I am going to send Victor there twice a week to begin this new treatment to see how it works. I'm quite hopeful that he will improve to the point where you can take him home, then the therapist would come to your home weekly. Your mother's piano is still there, isn't it? Or did that drunken man sell that too?"

"Ha! He tried, but Victor and I did not let him!"

"Yeah, he was a piece of work that man. I'm so pleased that he is gone for good, and that..."

Lilly is upset talking about him, so she cuts the doctor off and changes the topic, "You know, this does sound good for Victor, knowing his love for the classics – particularly piano. I'm sure he will see this new change as a sign of your approval, doctor. You know how much he values what you think." Then Lilly leans forward anxiously, "I am the only close family he has, and as my little brother he is all I have. Of course my relatives are great and have helped us through this tough time, but when you think of it, as a small family unit, we have only each other. Please help us get back to our life."

"You know that I am doing my best, but he has to help too." says the doctor.

"Okay, well let's begin and see what happens with this new therapy."

"Sounds good; though first we will have this introductory session tonight, just to see how Victor responds. If all goes well, we can begin with those two sessions a week."

"Good, I think it's a great idea! Have you talked to Victor?"

"I have briefly discussed how he feels about live piano music, and he seemed to respond positively to that. How about you talk to him and let him know more about the plan, and about the idea of two sessions a week. The therapist has only Mondays and Thursdays available for now. We'll take Victor tonight to Garden House to meet

Sebastian. Please talk to Victor and let me know before you go home."

"Great. I will!" She gets up to shake the doctor's hand, leaving his office with a big smile. She rushes back to Victor's room where he is lying on his bed, looking at the ceiling, buried in his thoughts. She sits on the bed, tickles him and asks what he is thinking. Victor sits up and looks at his sister impatiently, "What did he say? Is he angry with me?"

"Oh, no you silly. Actually he is planning a great program for you. Piano! Listening, or maybe even taking lessons if you want. What do you think?"

"Oh, so he knows that I didn't start the commotion?"

"Ah my sweet Victor, he's your doctor, and he knows that sometimes you cannot control your behaviour. But he also knows that most of the time you can, and that you are trying so hard. Now, get up and let's go downstairs to have your favourite breakfast so I can tell you all about it."

Victor gets up cheerfully, chattering happily as he walks, holding the hand of his sister, the only family he feels he has at this time. After breakfast, they leave the cafeteria to go for a walk around the rose garden near the beautiful Garden House. Lilly stays with him the whole morning, then leaves for the afternoon, though she promises Victor that she'll return for the evening meeting. She tells him that she'll be dressed up formally to meet the therapist. She asks Victor to have a nap and be fresh for the meeting. On her way out, she goes to the doctor's office to let him know that they will see him at six in Victor's room.

It is a quarter to six when the doctor enters Victor's room to walk with him to the appointment. Lilly hasn't arrived yet. Victor seems agitated, but soon Lilly appears and she gives him a big hug.

She shakes the doctor's hand saying, "Let's go, I am so excited about this new plan." The three of them leave the room and head toward Garden House.

The doctor asks Victor how he feels. Victor looks at him grimly, "You were watching me with your cameras, so you know what a great day I had."

The doctor and Lilly laugh out loud and Victor chuckles with them.

They arrive at Garden House and go inside. Many rooms are there with doors labelled Painting, Dance, Meditation, Theatre, and Music. They enter the music room where various musical instruments are arranged on long, solid shelves. A beautiful cherry-wood piano is in the corner. A young man is attending to it.

"Hello Sebastian." says the doctor.

"Hello doctor." He comes close and shakes the doctor's hand. The doctor introduces him to Lilly and Victor. Sebastian shakes their hands, then they all sit around a table and talk about Victor's interest in classical music. The doctor and the therapist are amazed with his knowledge about the different Masters.

Lilly is so proud of him. She says bashfully, "Our mother played classical music and taught us a few things."

Victor jumps in, "I learned a lot of the history of that music, and I listened to my mother teaching Lilly how to play. She played very well you know, but she's not playing any more. I am sad."

"Why are you sad?" the doctor asks.

"Well, she looks like my mother when she sits behind the piano, and she plays just like her. I enjoyed listening and watching her when she played. I'm just sad that she doesn't play anymore. Maybe she misses our mother. Why do you not play anymore Lilly?"

"Tonight is not about me, Victor. Let's talk about the plan," says Lilly with a serious look.

Sebastian asks Victor which, among all those Masters, is his favourite.

"Oh, Chopin and his Nocturnes; and among his Nocturnes, I prefer Op. 9, No.1. Can you play that? I always love to hear that live."

Sebastian looks at him with a smile, then gets up to sit at the piano and begin playing the requested Chopin piece. The beautiful, captivating melody fills the room as his fingers calmly and tenderly move over the keys. Lilly looks contently at her brother's happy face as the doctor quietly sits and observes.

Lilly thinks, *"He is so good. It is as if Chopin himself is playing; not that I ever met the gentleman."* She smiles at her silly thought, closing her eyes to listen.

After completing the piece, Sebastian sits quietly facing the piano for a few moments, then turns to Victor. "Well, what do you think? Did you like it?"

"I loved it! Do you know all Chopin's Nocturnes?"

"I do! And we will play a couple of them each time. What do you say?"

"I would love that! Thank you so much, sir!"

The doctor gets up, saying, "Well Lilly, let's go for a walk around the garden while these two gentlemen plan their sessions."

The two leave the room for a walk, then return in a half hour and sit in the living room. A few minutes later Victor and Sebastian join them. Victor's eyes are shining and he looks absolutely pleased. Lilly and the doctor exchange smiles of satisfaction. The plan is set for every Monday and Thursday at 6:00 pm for the next two months, with an evaluation after that.

This week is a quiet one for Victor. He stays in his room most of the time resting – listening to classical music; reading; thinking. He is anxiously waiting for the sessions to begin. He has promised Lilly, and himself of course, to learn, enjoy and co-operate so that he can go home as soon as possible. He is so happy to be working with this new therapist because he sees how just one meeting had such a wonderful effect on him.

The first session finally arrives, and Lilly pops in to see how Victor is doing. He has a new shirt on, complimenting himself in the mirror. Lilly hugs him tight and laughs.

"So, you conceited young man, are you ready?"

"Oh, I am and I cannot wait. I want to ask him to teach me as well. What do you think?"

"You never wanted to take lessons from mom; what is the change?"

"I was young and foolish. He played so beautifully. It was as if I was hearing Chopin himself. Also, mom will be happy and proud when I can play as nicely as her." They hold each other sadly as they remember their mother.

Lilly thinks dark thoughts, but realizes Victor should not be upset right before his first session, so she just messes up his hair saying, "Why are you dressed up so nicely? Planning to impress your therapist?"

"Yes, as well as my doctor. When they see I am well organized, perhaps Sebastian will more quickly agree to teach me as well. Then by the end of our two months of sessions, they will let me go home with you."

He looks at his watch and excitedly says, "I have to go now! Today I am going to ask him to play Chopin's Fantaisie Impromptu, Op. 66."

Lilly smiles at his eagerness and laughs at him, saying that it is nowhere near six o'clock yet. "From here to the house is not even a ten minute walk!"

Victor says, "I know, I know!" And he leaves anyway.

It is twenty minutes before the six o'clock appointment when Victor and Lilly arrive at Garden House. Of course they are way too early, so they check out the painting room for a while, enjoying its fascinating contents. They then go into the music room to admire the harmony and peacefulness of it. Victor looks anxious.

Lilly holds him tight, "You'll be fine. Oh, I hear voices in the living room, so I think it's time I left. Just relax and have fun."

In the living room Lilly finds the doctor and Sebastian talking.

"Oh, you are already here," says the doctor.

"Yes, we came early and were enjoying this marvellous house. Victor is in the room waiting for you."

Sebastian approaches her with a smile, and extends his hand in greeting. Lilly shakes it once and coldly says, "Hello, good to see you. Victor is in the room. I will wait here." Sebastian is a bit shocked at the curt response and exchanges a puzzled look with the doctor before going into music room.

Sebastian takes a nervous breath before he enters the room, but relaxes when he receives a warm and enthusiastic greeting from Victor. He sits at the piano to play several requests for Victor, who shows he knows his classical music. As they proceed with the session, Victor asks about including piano lessons in their time together, and if Sebastian can divide their meetings into two sessions: one for lessons, and the other for his therapy. Sebastian concedes that Victor has a good understanding of classical music and that he would likely learn quickly, so the session ends on a high note with a happy Victor, a satisfied doctor, an optimistic Lilly, and – off topic entirely – a keenly smitten Sebastian who cannot keep his eyes off Lilly's unassuming beauty.

The two months of trial therapy pass quickly. Sebastian is impressed with Victor's progress, and the doctor has noted how Victor is far less easily provoked to anger now. So they both agree that Victor should be able to leave the institution to live at home with Lilly, and that the sessions can continue, either in Sebastian's home or in their own home.

In Victor's room the four of them finalize plans, and then say their goodbyes.

In the hallway the doctor asks to see Sebastian in his office, where he cautions Sebastian about Lilly, telling him that he has noticed how he looks at Lilly affectionately.

"Well, I do like her very much. She is not my client, so there should be no problem. We are both single and she is only a few years younger than me. I don't know her well, but it seems we have a few little things here and there in common that we could build a relationship on." He pauses, and then says, "Although she's being a bit difficult. I always think I have done something wrong when I am around her."

"I'm glad you see that, actually," says the doctor. "Nothing is wrong with this situation, of course. However, Lilly has had a couple of bad experiences. They are linked to why Victor is here."

"What? Why? I am Victor's therapist; should I not know the history?"

"Well, I'm hesitant to go through the details of Lilly's life; however you are medically involved somewhat with this family, so yes you probably should know what you are getting into. Lilly's father, Alfred, was a very dear friend of mine. He was from England teaching economics here in Canada, and Lilly's mother, Sky, was from the Musqueam Nation. She was an English professor teaching at the same university as Alfred. They fell in love. They soon got married, had two children and a beautiful life together. But tragically the parents were killed in a car accident when Lilly was eighteen and Victor was ten.

"Victor was a minor and Lilly was not in a position to support herself and her brother, plus she was devastated and absolutely depressed. The family had been very intimate and loving. Losing both parents at once was not easy on them; particularly with Lilly as she was older and more sensitive, and she was dealing with a problem at the time for which she really needed her mother. Such a shame really; their loving family was just perfect – a dream. We all envied them. They were financially well off, had a nice house, and the two children were doing very well in school. After the accident, the children were placed with their Aunt River, Sky's sister. She locked the children's money away in a trust. She and her husband took care of them as if they were their own children. River even had their original house rented out, with the money going monthly into a new savings account for them.

"Lilly and Victor gradually settled into the new situation, but unfortunately a greedy and drunken uncle, the half-brother of Alfred, appeared from England saying he was here to take care of the children. He first accused their Aunt River of robbing the children's savings, but that clearly wasn't true, so then he tried a different tactic by claiming that the children were not getting proper education in a First Nations setting, and that they were living in an unhealthy environment. He even hired a private investigator that he paid off to falsify records. Long story short, after two years of fighting in court, he managed to take Victor and move him to his fancy apartment. Lilly moved in too to be with Victor. We all were devastated and none of us could understand why the judge gave custody of Victor to this unstable man. Over those two years, he was drunk most of the time. Even in court you could smell the alcohol when you talked to him. We really did not know what to do."

Sebastian is visibly upset. "What are you saying? There was documentation that their Aunt River was adding to the kids' savings, and taking good care of them both. Lilly was at an age to testify; why did the court listen to his nonsense?"

"Well, he used Lilly's depression and unstable behaviour. He even accused her of being licentious, and nobody said anything in that court to refute him. Remember that Sky, Lilly's mother, was pure First Nations, as was her whole family. Did you think the colonial law, which already had destroyed those people in so many ways, would consider them over a white man from England?"

"I cannot believe this," fumes Sebastian. "How, in this day and time, do things like this happen?"

"Well, part of the problem is that everyone is so busy with their daily lives that nobody pays attention to other matters in our society. Yes, it happens that courts will give a First Nations orphan child to a white family. And so in this case, yet again, the court sided with a foreign English man over a local First Nations family.

"That did not stop River though. Their aunt was all over their lives like a hawk. She had them visit her as much as she could, and she arranged outside activities as much as possible. She also documented anything she heard regarding the uncle's behaviour, and she taught Lilly how to do the same. As the months went by, they chronicled more and more of the drunken incidents, emotional abuse through shouting and name-calling, and inappropriate advances on Lilly.

"Over the next two years, the uncle kicked the tenant out of the house and moved them all there, thus losing an income. He managed money poorly, forcing Lilly to access her parents' savings.

"Finally, when Lilly was twenty-two and Victor was fourteen, River, along with a support group that I assembled, approached the court with enough evidence to arrange a hearing to revisit the custody question. When the uncle was served his summons to court, he was alone with Lilly and flew into a rage, accusing her of turning her "Indian" tribe against him. He grabbed her and began tearing off her clothes. Fortunately, Victor and his tutor arrived home at that time. Victor rushed at the uncle, pushing him away while the tutor ran to help Lilly and call the police. Victor and the uncle grappled and fought briefly in a desperate struggle that ended when the two of them knocked over a large cabinet, which fell on them. They were both unconscious when the police arrived. The three of them were taken to the hospital."

Sebastian is breathless and frantically asks the doctor, "What? She went to the hospital too? He raped Lilly? Oh my!"

"No, no, he did not succeed before the tutor and Victor arrived, but she was bruised and battered enough to require a precautionary examination. So, Lilly still was physically lucky for the second time."

"What do you mean for the second time?"

"Well, when she graduated from high school, she was at an after-party where she was assaulted by a boy on drugs who dragged her violently into a corner. But before he could rape her a couple of her friends arrived, beat the crazy boy off, and took the frantic Lilly to hospital. Her parents were on their way to the hospital when they had that accident and died. Lilly was totally devastated with the loss of her parents and, as I said, it was just at a time when she needed her mother so much."

"O boy, no wonder she is so aloof. I understand now why she can seem so cold and distant. Thanks for sharing this."

"Yes, it's best to be careful around her. She has had bad experiences and has stayed away from relationships with men."

Sebastian looks at the doctor gloomily, listening with full attention as he continues.

"Now, as you have read in Victor's hospital files, he was unconscious for three weeks and he had two deep cranial contusions on his head. By the time he woke up, the stitches were out and the wounds were healing well. However, he could not talk, read or write. He had a very bad headache that caused him to have tantrum episodes. He was confused and did not know anyone at first, even Lilly. After several months of medication, and after two operations for removing a blood clot and stopping some persistent internal bleeding, he slowly got to the point where he could recognize Lilly, and then their Aunt River

– and soon after that most others one by one. I have worked with him ever since he recovered from his physical injuries and could talk, read and write again.

"That incident was four years ago. Over this period of time, many people worked with Victor to keep improving his condition. I have had him at my clinic since last year, during which time he has improved steadily, and now with your help he is improving even more and will be whole again, hopefully soon."

"What happened to that drunken man, the uncle?" asks Sebastian.

"He woke up in hospital the same day and was arrested right there. He tried to work the system any way he could to get himself back to England, but we all helped out again by supporting River. She worked hard challenging the uncle and the system, and we didn't allow him to get away with anything, despite River's limited influence as a First Nations woman. He was a piece of work, that man. Don't worry; he can never be a menace anymore. Before his trial began, he had a heart attack and died."

"Oh, what tragedies these two have had to face. I am so sorry to hear all this. So yes, I must be much more sensitive with Lilly. You know, I thought she dislikes me because I am kind of white. I did not know her beloved father was an English man."

"No, Lilly is not prejudiced that way. But she says she is going to live single forever, so she tends to be cold with all men. You may have a difficult time with her, so make sure you do not cause more problems. The good thing is that Victor is so fond of you, and thriving. Let's focus on that for now."

"Okay, no worries. I'll do my best with Victor, and I'll be careful with Lilly. But just so you know," Sebastian says with a smile as he gets up to leave the doctor's office, "I won't give up on Lilly. I think I'm falling for her. I will do my best to have her attention."

The doctor ponders on his own for a while then smiles positively as he prepares to leave for home himself. "Do your best young man, you are good for her."

The sessions progress steadily. Victor is so happy that he is learning piano. He likes his instructor-therapist very much, as Sebastian is kind and patient. They have developed a good relationship, to the point where Sebastian is becoming a little like a father figure to Victor. He has noticed Sebastian's caring behaviour towards his sister, which makes him happy; he imagines that if Lilly likes Sebastian, then they can all be friends for life. However, Victor also notices Lilly's aloofness towards Sebastian.

He tries to talk to his sister about how Sebastian seems to like her, and how positive he is for both of them, but Lilly always cuts him off with something like, "Stop! I don't care about what you are thinking. You and I will live together, the two of us. We have Aunt River and the rest of the family, so we do not need anyone else."

Victor would argue, "What do you mean we will always live together? What if I meet someone and want to have a family of my own?"

At that point she might smile and say, "That would be wonderful! When that happens, you and your family can live in the house and I will get my own place; and that is end of the discussion."

As the weeks and months go by, Sebastian makes his visits as carefree as possible. Sometimes he brings along a nice pastry or a small gift for Victor; oh, and something for Lilly too while he was at it – maybe a good book or some favourite music. The presents are not expensive or fancy, but they usually align well with what Sebastian is learning about Lilly's preferences and style.

At least once a week, Sebastian and Victor plan a day trip or a picnic for the three of them, or Sebastian takes them out to dinner. During these pleasant outings, Lilly and Victor learn more about Sebastian's past. His father was born and raised in Spain where he met and fell in love with a French-Canadian woman. They married, had Sebastian, then after two years they came to Canada where his two siblings were born. He always talks about his family with deep love and respect. He has many funny stories of his childhood in Montréal that make Lilly and Victor laugh.

Lilly comes to feel more and more comfortable around Sebastian, not least of all because of her appreciation of how quickly Victor is improving as a result of his music therapy. She enjoys sitting behind Sebastian when he plays piano, watching his back and the delicate movements in his shoulders. She also likes his long curly black hair, and the way he holds his head as he plays.

Soon it comes to be that if she hasn't seen Sebastian for a few days, she gets agitated and asks Victor, "Don't you guys have sessions anymore?"

Then Victor typically replies, "No Lilly, we are done. I'm doing my courses at adult school, remember? Have you hit your head somewhere? It's over a month since our therapy sessions ended. Just him being in my life, teaching me piano, and being my friend; those are the best therapies for me at this point."

"Sure, sure, I know. Sorry to bother you; and you do not have to be snippy with me."

"And you don't need to be so hard-headed. Admit you have missed him – that you have feelings for him. Why can't you see how great he is? You blind woman!" Victor mumbles as he walks away.

She realizes at such times that she misses Sebastian's warm velvety voice and his loving gazes that flick away when she catches him looking. She doesn't want him to shy away. She wonders to herself if this is love. Yet she is scared, and for reasons that she doesn't want to explore, she resists him.

Two years pass this way with the three of them spending much of their time together. Sebastian works around their house, repairing the banister, fixing lights, doing anything else to help. Victor and Lilly sometimes go to Sebastian's for dinner. They are together most weekends, and they take short trips or stay over at one of the houses. The three of them sometimes visit Lilly and Victor's aunts and the rest of the family, who all seem to like Sebastian very much. Lilly has graduated and has a good job. Victor is doing very well in school. Sebastian has completed his PhD and is looking for a different job. He knows Lilly is fond of him, so he doesn't hide his own feelings as much anymore. He cares for her very much, something she is quite well aware of now.

One night after dinner, Victor is practicing his piano lessons. Sebastian comments on how he really does not need any more lessons. He closes his eyes to appreciate Victor's music for a while, and then turns to Lilly. He asks her to dance with him. She smiles and accepts. They dance gracefully to the slow melody, Sebastian always keeping his distance and letting Lilly initiate.

But tonight, toward the end of the piece, he does lean in close enough to whisper in her ear, "Let me love you."

Lilly pulls herself back, looks into his eyes deeply for a while, then smiles and puts her head on his shoulder. Sebastian is so thrilled that breathing becomes difficult for him. But he gets his act together and continues dancing, caressing Lilly's beautiful long black hair.

Victor's face is the picture of delight as he watches this scene. He continues playing with a happy grin on his face. He finishes the piece and sits watching as Sebastian and Lilly still move slowly. He chuckles and says, "Hey love birds, to what are you dancing?"

They stop. Lilly looks at Sebastian once, then quickly turns and goes to her room. Sebastian messes Victor's hair and says, "Way to spoil my moment, man."

"Sorry, I thought she would be okay with a little teasing."

They sit by the fire for a while, but when she doesn't return Sebastian looks upset.

"That's fine, young man." says Sebastian. He gets up to leave. "Perhaps she was tired and fell asleep. I'm tired too. Good night and see you in a few days."

After he leaves, Victor goes to his sister's door and knocks.

"Come in," says Lilly. Victor opens the door to find her in the dark standing at the window, watching as Sebastian drives away. He joins her at the window.

"Why did you leave?"

"I don't know Victor. I know that I love this kind and sensitive man very much, but I don't know how to deal with him and my own feelings."

Victor holds her, then whispers, "He's not like any man I have ever met, and he is in love with you."

After a few minutes Lilly says, "I know, and I like it very much."

Victor kisses her head and says, "I'm sure you will find a way to respond. I know you love him too."

Lilly blushes and admits that she does love him. She pauses a bit and says, "We've been going to each other's houses for about two years, right?"

"Yes, why you are asking this?"

"Well, I remember when we began to go to his home he gave us a tour. We could go everywhere, in any room. But recently I see that as soon as we arrive he closes his bedroom door. Do you know why?"

"I do know, but you have to see it for yourself. I am going to his home next week, because we're planning to build a desk for me. You come too. I'll keep him busy in the workshop while you go see what he is hiding there."

"What? I would never do that; this is discourteous!"

"Okay. Suit yourself." And he leaves her room smiling mischievously. Lilly sits in the dark. She smiles at her clever brother, as curiosity chews away at her.

The day arrives for Victor and Sebastian to enjoy some carpentry work. Lilly goes with Victor, though she is not comfortable. She says hello to Sebastian bashfully and avoids looking into his eyes. Sebastian has everything ready in the workshop. He rubs his hands together. "Okay Victor, let's go make a nice desk for you."

Lilly says, "I will make you two hard-working men some cool drinks." Victor smiles as he watches his sister disappear into the kitchen.

There, Lilly makes lots of noise for a while – "making a cool drink" – then cautiously returns to the living room. She looks at the closed bedroom door, and while listening for the sounds of activity in the workshop, she approaches the door murmuring, "Why do you close this door on me Sebastian – only this door?" With a nervous hand she slowly opens the door to a room darkened by drawn window drapes. She turns the light on, and breathes in sharply when she sees the wall above his desk. It is covered in photos of her, like wallpaper. They are scenes from their many outings such as their forest walks, mountain climbs, dinners and swims in lakes and rivers. She sees the day they were on a picnic, and she was playfully chasing butterflies when a colourful one sat down on her hand and she laughed so cheerfully. The most amazing photo shows her as she was jumping into a lake; another shows her playing with Victor; another shows a beautiful peaceful scene in the rose garden near the Garden House, around the time Victor was doing his therapy sessions. She remembers that many of their beautiful moments together were captured, but only her photos are on the wall above his desk. There is also a single photo of her by his bedside. She looks around and sadly thinks, *"Wow, these pictures go all the way back to when we first met! How much I made this man suffer. How respectful he was all this time. I couldn't even guess that he loved me from the beginning. How sweet. What should I do? How do I tell him that I love him too? I don't know what to do or say."*

She turns to rush out of the room, but catches sight of Sebastian's clothes folded on the bed and his luggage bags open on the sofa and floor, as if he is preparing to go somewhere. Puzzled, she again turns to leave the room, but realizes Victor and Sebastian are at the door. She looks down, embarrassed.

Victor is upset that he helped put his sister in this situation and leaves to go back to the workshop.

Sebastian comes closer, holds her hand and, taking her chin, lifts up her face. They look at each other for a bit. She says, "I am so sorry for being so difficult. I don't know what to say or do. I have never been with anyone."

"It's okay. I know. I have loved you all along and was just waiting for you to love me back."

"Where are you going?" Lilly asks anxiously.

"Well, I wanted to tell you two today. I have received a very promising invitation to be part of a research group at Geneva University. I want to stay there for some time." He pauses, then says, "Maybe when I'm not around, you can deal with your feelings better. Then perhaps one day you can tell me that you love me too.”

“No, no. Don't go, please.”

“Why not?” Sebastian asks sadly. “It didn’t seem you cared about my feelings for you, so I thought it best for me to start anew somewhere else.”

“Don't say that. You know that I care about you. I think I even have feelings for you too, and you know that.”

“But you cannot talk about your feelings or let me in. Come on, Lilly; it’s so hard for me. I don’t know if you will ever let me in, or if we can ever have a future together.” Then in a very low and affectionate tone he says “You know how much I love you; I cannot breathe or relax if I don't see enough of you. But when we are together, I have to constantly watch what I am saying or doing to avoid making you angry or sad. I don't know what to do. I love you; I want to be with you. But not like this. If you have feelings for me, tell me; talk about it. Why can't you tell me? Haven't I earned your trust yet?"

He is standing in the middle of the room looking passionately and lovingly at Lilly. She looks at him from behind a veil of tears, and smiles at him. Sebastian takes her hands in his, but then quickly pulls back and says, "What is it? Why you are shivering and shaking? What did I say? Oh, I didn't mean to upset you. I'm sorry!"

Lilly puts a finger on his lips, holds his hand, walks with him to the sofa, and asks him to sit. Sebastian sits down speechless because she has never touched him like this before. She stands looking down at him. After a few agonizing moments, she says, "Don't say a word. Do not interrupt me, and do not touch me; just let me say what I have to say."

Sebastian just nods and waits apprehensively.

Lilly is no less flustered, but after a few more minutes, she slowly moves closer to Sebastian and gently sits on his lap. Sebastian hardly breathes; he just stares at her without moving. She takes his right arm and positions it around her body. She then takes a deep breath, moving his left arm onto her lap. She shifts herself into a comfortable position in his arms and on his lap, then takes another deep breath. Blushing, she takes Sebastian's face in her hands and smiles at him tenderly, though nervously. She looks into his eyes for a few minutes, as they both breathe deeply. She then calmly reaches for his lower lip taking it to her mouth, and with a tender bite says, "Lilly," then takes his upper lip and says, "loves," and releases it, then moves closer to put both her lips on his and says, "Sebastian."

She then pulls back. "You know I love you very much, but it is so difficult for me to talk about my feelings. I have never been with anyone, and I do not know what to do. You have to let me practice. I love you and I want to spend my life with you. You are the best thing that ever happened to me – and to Victor, of course."

She takes a deep breath, continuing, "Before I met you, I believed I would live my life alone, and for years I shut everyone out." She pauses for a few moments then says, "I think I was waiting for you all along, and I always had an image of a man like you in my mind. So there, I said it."

Sebastian sits quietly, blissfully savouring that romantic and beautiful way of saying, "I love you".

Lilly smiles at him. "Well? Are you still leaving the city?"

They look at each other passionately as Sebastian caresses her face and neck with his fingers, then reaches for her lips just the same way Lilly did and kisses them one by one. He then kisses her nose and her chin and her ears, and with each he says word by word, "I", "love", "you", "so", "much"... And then says softly, "I would love to spend my life with you."

Lilly looks into his eyes, "I know," and then puts her head on his chest releasing herself into his arms.

After a few minutes sitting quietly, Sebastian reaches for Lilly's hand, kisses it, then puts Lilly's hand on his own chest. He says, "We are going to explore and practice love and love making, but I'll always be learning my limits. How about we use this as your safety signal; you always have your hand just like this on my chest, and if I pass that limit, you push me back. What do you say?" He takes Lilly's chin, brings her face close to his, and kisses her forehead and repeats, "What do you say?"

Lilly smiles, looking at him behind that veil of tears and nods. Sebastian kisses her eyes and holds her tight.

After a few minutes he says, "Would you like to go out for a bite?"

"Sure, but after you unpack your stuff."

Sebastian gets up as he holds her, lifting her up like a child. He turns around the room laughing happily, and kisses her cheek. He sets her gently down and says, "As you wish, my lady. But wouldn't you like to go with me? We can have a new beginning over there, the three of us!"

"You mean we all go there? What would I do there?"

"Go to school, or be my research assistant, or just have fun around the city. Whatever you like!"

Victor is bored and fed up with waiting in the workshop. He comes back into the house to see what is going on, arriving just at the moment Lilly laughs and says, "I would love to go with you to Switzerland. It would be a great adventure!"

"What? Who is going where? What about me?"

Lilly and Sebastian laugh and hug him. Sebastian says, "Never without you, Victor my friend! Because of you we found each other, and we will all stick together; unless you don't want to come!"

"Oh no, I will definitely go with you guys. You cannot get rid of me by giving me options!"

The house is filled with laughter. Lilly is restless between the two people she cares for more than anything. With cheerful banter, they get ready to leave the house to go have dinner, plan their trip, and begin their lives together.

RACISM

I have learned through my life that racism is a word that describes negative interactions between peoples. These are rooted in economic distresses, historical political power relationships, personal power relationships, and simple misunderstandings. It is not just concerned with newcomers to a country, but is something that also exists within a country among peoples who have lived together for generations. For instance, the problems and tensions found between French and English Canadians are similar to issues that I saw in Iran among Kurds, Turks, and Fars (Persians).

As a child I heard all kinds of racist jokes about Turks. Of course, Turks had jokes about Kurds, and Kurds had jokes about Turks, and Fars were aloof, and had jokes for both. Turks were senseless, and Kurds were vicious. My father always said Turks come to the city and bring disorder and chaos and too many children; or the Kurds are nice people but why don't they stay in their own area. He didn't know or understand that they came because of economic factors, such as a lack of jobs, poor drinking water, an inadequate health system, and many more problems in their own areas. The regions where Turks and Kurds lived were economically distressed, and moving to Tehran was only natural as a way to improve their lives.

I moved to Greece soon after the revolution in Iran. There I learned that the Greeks have an enormous hatred for Turks. Why? Turks occupied their country for 400 years and even though that historical imperialist victimization ended two centuries ago, new generations of Greeks feel entitled to hate new generations of Turks who had nothing to do with it. Racist hatred seems to have a long-lasting attraction that can maintain itself long after the events that engendered it.

I soon started to do some research into where in the world I might settle for good. I learned from other friends and family who had already settled in Sweden and northern Europe that they called us Black Heads there. I heard that Australia was assumed to be the most racist country of all, and that in Germany people threw hot water on refugees who were protesting in front of the UN for their status. I was worried that racists were everywhere. Where should I go?

Eventually I decided to consider Canada, hearing that it is better than other places. A year after my arrival, I entered college where I was relieved to encounter no racism personally. Upon graduation, I began work as a computer programmer. One day, I returned from my break to find my telephone missing from my desk. As my job involved constant communication with clients, the phone was vital. A quick survey determined that everybody else still had their phones, yet mine was gone.

Inquiries were met with what seemed to be cowed silence, but one brave friend whispered that the Project Manager had taken it. As I approached her, I heard her say something along the lines of, "she comes from the Sahara, and now she wants a phone." Her response to my challenge about my missing phone was, "Don't worry about it, you don't need it." My manager immediately made her return my phone and apologize to me, but I will never forget the humiliation and pain she put me through while I worked there.

Now, how am I to analyze this incident? To me, there was a definite element of racism involved. But why did she act on her feelings. Did she feel insecure with this new, young, foreign, energetic, fast-paced lady in her sphere of influence? It would seem she felt she had to project her personal power over the situation, and I had to suffer for it.

Years passed, and I moved to Vancouver, and eventually changed my field from computers to

Psychology. I started working at a Women's Centre, using my computer background and English abilities to teach ESL plus computer skills to new immigrants.

One day, I was invited to a workshop about Hidden Racism and how to deal with it. In attendance were over 50 ladies from many cultural backgrounds: Indigenous, French and English Canadian, Iranian, African, Arab, Indian, Oriental, etc. After introducing ourselves and talking about experiences of racism, one of the English ladies leading the session distributed some hand-outs as discussion aids, then asked all the "white" women to remain in the room, while the coloured women were to go to the meeting room downstairs. I couldn't quite believe what I heard, but the speaker assured us that there was a purpose to the segregation. Not wanting to be overly-hasty in my judgment, I went downstairs and listened patiently to the discussions.

At the end of the session, no obvious reason was given for separating the group based on race except the excuse that white women have different racist issues than coloured women. I told the leader that if the workshop was supposed to be about racism, then we should all be together as citizens of the same world facing the same problems to share our knowledge and experiences, and work out solutions jointly. "What are you teaching about racism if you don't even sit at the same table in the same room with us?" I then left, as did about half of the other women in attendance.

The organizers of that workshop surely had no intention of displaying any racist behavior. But their inappropriate use of breaking into groups showed a lack of understanding of how segregation looks to people who are sensitive to such activity.

I have traveled from the Middle East to Greece, Turkey, Germany, England, France, Canada and the U.S. I can share many stories of racism, but the issue is not a simple one of just one group hating another group. It is deeply rooted in historical memory, in the economic wealth and welfare of people, and in the struggle to understand each other and our world.

Neo: New, revived

A Dog's Life in Iran
versus the West

All my life I had been taught to fear and hate dogs. Then, to my surprise, I learned that I could love one! Somehow, I changed from believing that dogs are unclean brutes not fit to live with people, to being a dog lover who cares for a beautiful little creature that follows me everywhere and is as fond of me as I am of him. How did this happen?

In my native culture, dogs are assumed to be the dirtiest, filthiest and nastiest of creatures. People never allow them into their homes; in fact, it is believed that animals and people should not live in the city together. Farmers and shepherds in the countryside use dogs as tools, but in the city, they are chased by kids on the street and hit with sticks and stones. I always felt mildly sorry for the animals and could never join in the sport, but I was never outraged by their treatment – no one was.

There was one dog in our neighbourhood that had a few puppies. Neighbourhood kids hit her because she had eaten a couple of her puppies. Who would do such a thing they said, and they beat her up some more. My heart ached – I can still hear her howling to this day. I thought she must be hungry if she would eat her children; I thought that if I fed her she wouldn't do it again. One evening, I got some meat and potatoes then snuck out to try to feed her. She was scared of me and I was scared of her, so I threw the food at her. This continued for a few nights, until my father found out about it and I was punished. I think he called the city, because we didn't see her anymore.

In 1985 I left Iran, moving to Greece for a couple of years. There I felt confirmed in my belief that dogs are dirty and filthy. In Athens many people had dogs, but there was no law or cultural rule about cleaning up after them. Feces were everywhere on the sidewalk and in the parks where children played. I found that disgusting. I could no longer walk with my head up and look at the sky, the buildings, or the flowers around me; instead my eyes were always on the ground on the lookout for poop. It was a wonder to me that people could live with that filth everywhere.

I then came to Canada where I saw a more balanced approach. Dogs were well loved but their "effects" were kept under control and not permitted to contaminate the urban environment. I liked that; however, it was still a mystery to me that dogs could be accepted into homes. For instance, a few years after my arrival in Canada, I heard the lady who was working in the cubical next to me sobbing. I asked what the matter was. She said that her dog had passed away after thirteen years of companionship. I don't remember what I said to her, but I remember leaving her cubical thinking, *"These people are crazy; she cries as if her father had died."*

Years passed, and soon my daughter, born and raised in Canada, was asking for a dog because all her friends had them. With real trepidation, I accepted a little toy poodle into my house. It didn't take long, though, before I came to understand the affection and companionship that came with him. It was during this time that my father passed away in Iran, and though I was naturally upset, I knew that I would be equally upset when our little Neo passed on. I can now completely relate to the lady in my office who had lost her loving, affectionate friend. As with my dog, hers was always there to love her unconditionally.

The appearance of Neo was a cultural shock to my Iranian family and friends, and some of them never got used to him, no matter how much I tried to explain that dogs are not necessarily dirty or filthy. It is up to us how we take care of our hygiene and theirs.

Here in Canada, dogs live with people and are treated like their children. I can now accept this fact. Conversely in Iran, they were never loved like a member of the household. Nevertheless, I hear that recently some people are adopting the dog as a pet in Tehran. This is not going over well with the tradition-bound, conservative government there. It has passed laws forbidding dogs from being in public. That is not surprising in a country that treats its people as badly as those kids in my childhood treated that vagrant dog.

Years passed, and I grew to love my Neo more. He became attached to me as his pack leader or mother. In the twelve years we had Neo, we grew accustomed to some of his behaviours. For instance, if he was hungry or needed something, he would come and sit right in front of me, staring at me for as long as was necessary for me to clue in that he had a request. Or if he needed to go outside, he would go to the back door and sit there patiently, waiting for one of us to see him. Sometimes he wanted me to hold him. When I did, he would put his head on my arm, face up, and stare at me to remind me that it was singing time. I sang for him as he looked into my eyes. I could see that he felt the emotion; and we were one at that moment.

I loved him as much as my children, but as I never thought that a dog may have pain or problems, perhaps I did not take care of him as I did my children. I cleaned his teeth and gave him his yearly checkup, but I never followed up concerning his excessive panting. He would do this as soon as he got in the car. When I asked around everyone said, ah, all dogs pant. Well, no they don't, not like that. So, for this careless behaviour, I lost him in 2012. I lost him to a congenital heart problem, which I had never known was the cause of all that panting. He is gone and a part of me is gone with him.

Lori: Laurel tree, or symbolic of honour and victory

Pamoon: Aware, Sensitive, (Cree)

Abebe: Flourishing (Ethiopian)

PARADISE OF THE
DOWNCASTS

It is almost twelve midnight. She is tired, her feet are numb, and her back is hurting. *"In about ten minutes I will be out of here,"* she thinks as she begins cleaning up, hoping that nobody comes into the store.

Right at twelve she turns on the "Closed" sign then turns off the front light. She finishes up the cleaning, turns off the remaining lights, locks the door and drags her exhausted body toward the bus stop. Tonight she is on time, but for the past couple of nights she has missed the last bus and had to walk over an hour to get home. Tom, her husband, couldn't believe her customers could be so inconsiderate as to take their sweet time in walking around the store, buying sweets, pop and cigarettes, and leisurely chit-chatting right at closing time. He was angry. They had yet another fight, which woke up the kids.

Lori is only thirty-eight years old, though she looks somewhat older as the mechanisms of hardship have put a nice map of crow's-feet on her face. She is nonetheless very pretty, and until recently had a successful career. A smart and talented student, she had graduated from secondary school with honours and immediately entered college where she completed an electronics degree. Within a year she had found an excellent job at an electronics company, with a decent wage and good benefits.

She met Tom at work, they fell in love, and six months later were married. The first three years were a honeymoon. Soon they had two children together who grew up happy, smart and healthy. Tom and Lori are proud of their kids. Joy is now ten, and Jade is eight.

Then, three years ago, the company they both worked for declared bankruptcy… but of course not before paying out fat bonuses to the CEO and top executives. That selfish action put over 300 employees on the street – people who had families and obligations – leaving them jobless and confused.

Tom and Lori, like most of the others, had many difficulties as they searched fruitlessly for similar employment. Unable to find jobs to match their skills, Tom ended up working at a gas station, while Lori obtained work in a franchised convenience store. From six-figure salaries, their wages went down to around ten or twelve dollars per hour. Not being able to pay their mortgage, they soon lost their home. Debts began to pile up.

Struggling to survive day in and day out, Tom and Lori haven't the energy or opportunity to learn another trade, and because they are unable to stay current in their own professions, finding jobs similar to what they had previously is not going to be easy.

Lori knows that when Tom picks a fight, it is mainly out of frustration. He regrets it right away and apologizes. Nevertheless, Lori is tired of the fighting. She is working hard, is worried for their future and those of their children, and she knows the fighting can only weaken their relationship.

She arrives home deep in her sad thoughts, but before she can put the key in the door, Tom opens it, takes her bag, and holds her tight. He kisses her fondly as they walk into the living room together. Lori is surprised. "What is going on? You seem so happy?"

"Of course I am; I just received a job offer. Finally, one of the many résumés I sent out responded. I did not tell you earlier because I wanted to be sure. I didn't want to have our hopes up like the last two times, only to have them dashed. Remember how sad we were for some time after they turned me down. This time I have signed a contract and I'll be working full time as of tomorrow: a proper salary and better benefits!"

He hugs her again, cheerfully declaring, "Things are going to be better!"

Lori laughs and cries at the same time, and they sit down together for a glass of wine as Tom fills her in on the details of his new job: maintaining robots which do assembly work.

However, Tom is still worried, not knowing if he can keep this job. "I don't know how long it will take before smarter robots make me redundant too, along with a few others there."

Lori sits back with her wine, frowning. "Well, isn't that ironic! Automation is partly why we lost our last jobs. Wow, it has been a tough three years. At times we didn't eat properly, we haven't been able to enrol the kids in any sports activities or camps lately, and they are always wearing the same old clothes, to the point where their shirts and pants are an embarrassment. But still they say nothing, and they never complain."

She continues heatedly, "Am I upset with new labour-saving systems and robotics? Am I down on technology? Of course not, but I'm so disappointed that we humans cannot put the same effort into arranging society, so that everyone has a livable wage, as we do into making robots designed to take away our jobs. If one day robots handle every task, then what are we going to do? Who is going to pay our expenses? Do we have any plan for that day? Or are we only focusing on having the best and smartest machines, giving no thought to the army of jobless people?"

Tom holds her tight, "These are important things to discuss, but for now don't worry. I have this job and summer is approaching. We'll be able to buy our precious ones some new clothes and put them both into summer camps of their choice."

Lori agrees. After talking a bit more they go to bed to rest their exhausted bodies. Early the next morning, Tom gets up to head out to his new job, leaving Lori to lie in bed thinking. Eventually she goes to the kitchen to help her children with breakfast and with packing their lunches, before kissing them and sending them off to school.

Knowing she has another shift in the afternoon, she begins cleaning her house, doing the laundry, and preparing food for when her children get home from school. By two in the afternoon she gets ready for work then walks to the bus stop, thinking, "*I do not see enough of my kids; when I go home they are sleeping, and I only get a few minutes with them in the morning and maybe one day on the weekend."* She sighs as she waits for her bus. It begins to rain. She takes a deep breath to feed her lungs with the fresh smell of wet leaves and rich soil.

Her shift begins at three o'clock, but she gets there ten minutes early to talk a bit with Francis before she leaves. "How is your daughter, Francis?"

"She's the same, if not worse. The second round of chemo wore her down a lot. She is very weak and so tired, and in such pain that she doesn't care if she lives or dies."

Francis cries as she talks about her seventeen-year-old child who is being eaten up by cancer. Lori holds her and asks if there is anything she can do. Francis kindly thanks her, "Oh, you have already done a lot. Thanks for covering me today; and the books you gave her are wonderful. My baby likes those very much, thanks!"

They hug each other as she leaves work to go to the hospital and attend to her daughter.

Lori takes her place behind the cash register just as Abebe arrives. He is another worker there, a very polite and quiet Ethiopian man who spends his break time reading. He reads on the bus too, and any other chance he gets. His co-workers call him Mr. Bookworm; he smiles, saying nothing.

Then Pamoon arrives, and as soon as she sees Lori she gives her a big smile, "I didn't know you were working today. Good to see you!"

"Well, I took Francis' shift, so she could go to the hospital."

"So nice of you! How is her daughter?"

"Not well, though the doctors say with this new round of chemo she should be better."

"I say she will be gone with this round of chemo," says Abebe. "She has no energy anymore; her body is so weak and fragile."

Pamoon agrees, as the three of them shake their heads over Francis's ordeal. As Abebe stocks shelves he explains how chemotherapy targets the bad tumour cells, but also harms many healthy cells, making some organs weak and vulnerable.

"Chemotherapy works against active cells, which are cells that are growing and dividing into more of the same type of cell. Cancer cells are active, but some normal cells may be affected by the drugs some. With her first full round of chemo, her body has weakened and needs time to recover. She had radiation treatment too, didn't she?"

"Yes, that's true. I think that was the very first treatment," says Lori.

Abebe shakes his head and says, "Which could be the cause of her second cancer. She has now two types of cancer, right?"

Pamoon looks at him suspiciously, "How do you know all this?"

"I was a doctor in Ethiopia: a specialist as well as a surgeon. I dealt with many cancer patients. I came to Canada under the skilled worker immigration program, yet as soon as I arrived here they basically deskilled me. I couldn't find work in my profession because I didn't have a Canadian degree, nor did I have any Canadian experience. The government would have known this from the beginning, so what does that mean? Do they intend to make low wage labourers out of professionals?"

Abebe opens some boxes and continues, "As for experience, that's the funniest part, because professionals in the medical field all have the same experience. Don't all people have the same organs and body parts, and more or less the same illnesses all across the world? In fact, where I am from, there are more illnesses, therefore physicians there actually have more experience. I can assure you I am much more qualified than many doctors here because in Ethiopia we deal with more complicated diseases than here, not to mention war wounds, as well as the usual conditions you would find anywhere in the world. You see how I am studying all the time; that's because I'm getting ready to do a whole series of redundant tests just to become a Canadian physician."

With a downcast face he finishes stocking the shelves. "I am quite upset and regret coming here, but I have no choice anymore. I have nowhere to go. Well, I'll tell you what I know now; my country needs me, and Ethiopians need me. I am trying to get my job back in the hospital where I used to work, and if I get it I will return home. It is so unfair, because my family paid a lot for my education there, and now here I am paying again for doing the same tests that I have already done. I don't understand why they give us visas when they know we cannot work here in our professions."

He sighs and quietly walks away into the stockroom, leaving Lori and Pamoon looking at each other in awe.

A customer arrives at the cash to pay for her purchase, so Lori attends to her while Pamoon goes into the stockroom to help Abebe sort through the new shipments. They work quietly, with Pamoon looking at his gloomy face from time to time.

The store is quiet for now, and Lori joins them in their work, eventually breaking the silence, "You know Abebe, we can actually relate somewhat to your situation. We are not doing so well here either, because the whole dysfunctional economic system imposes hardships on so many hard-working citizens all around the world. Everything is set up so the maximum number of people are serving the fewest number of wealthy opportunists. I too had a decent job, but the owners of the company, after dividing up the wealth of our labour, announced bankruptcy and left over 300 workers on the street. We lost our home, and our children are suffering as we cannot provide enough for their needs, even though my husband and I are both working hard. We all know how everything is now more expensive; what we make does not compensate for our needs. So, we are not happy either."

Pamoon shakes her head, "Well, I am from the Cree nation and you probably have heard how my people were living in tune with nature, using resources appropriately and mostly in harmony with the Earth. Then Europeans arrived to kill, destroy, and displace the nations, all the while calling *us* the savages. They forced us onto reserves and, needless to say, I am sure you have heard about the conditions many First Nations people are living in on reserves today. My parents worked hard to send me to school so that I could have a better life than the one they had. They supported me up until three years ago, but then my father passed away and my mother fell ill and could not work. That left me to work here full time and take the rest of my courses one at a time to complete my program to get my bachelor's degree.

"And how about my brother; he got a degree as a lab technician. He began working for a government research facility. There, discrimination and bullying at work bothered him so much that he quit his job. Later, he signed up with Doctors Without Borders and now works with a team in Africa. Imagine that; his rightful homeland, in which our people lived for thousands of years, is here! And yet we are still pushed around and live with many difficulties."

Pamoon continues, "Anyway, each of our cases is just a specific instance that points to a much larger issue. I don't think it has so much to do with me being First Nation and you being African. Look at Lori and her husband with their European background. Today we are all working hard for our day-to-day necessities just like they do in the struggling nations. Don't forget, here we are living in a country with one of the best standards of living on this planet, yet so many people face so many difficulties."

"Yes, and do you know what the tragedy is here?" says Abebe. "The system has been set up to profit just a few people, while many across the world work hard within this framework, without properly understanding it.

Individualism is encouraged so that everyone cares only for the self and nobody else. People everywhere work hard to achieve and live The American Dream, which is just to get rich no matter how and no matter what harm it causes. Consequently, they spend little time learning and understanding what is going on around them. They continue to contribute to a system that hurts them the most."

"Yes, I couldn't agree more," a strong voice says.

The three of them turn to the door where a tall, well-built man smiles at them kindly. "I overheard your very interesting conversation. Sorry, I couldn't help it. You are all correct. The systems all across the world were set by the rich, formed and shaped for the rich, and designed so that they can control their fellow citizens and convince them that their unjust incomes are fair. Then they declare that if you want to have what they have, you just need to work harder. So we accept their theory, their sick theory of individualism, and end up doing little more than catering to the wishes of the power-hungry, as the vicious cycle of poverty all the while destroys lives."

The friendly customer smiles and chuckles, "What a beautiful gathering: a Caucasian, an African, a First Nation, and here I am, an African-American."

Pamoon laughs with him and says, "It seems we all know the problems, but what do we do about it, and how are we challenging them?"

Abebe says, "By learning more; talking; educating ourselves and others. As for me, I will do my best to go back home and work for people who need me and appreciate me."

Pamoon puts her hand on Abebe's shoulder, "Ah, you're right. You have found your way, and I'm happy for you. As for me, I have taken to preaching among my people that the best way to heal is to challenge the unmerited system and force it to change. I tell them that when they see the positive changes from their efforts, it will give them a great feeling of accomplishment thus helping much faster in the healing."

The customer chuckles with joy, "You guys are an awesome bunch. I should come here more often. Now, which one of you smart ones would like to help me at the cash?" They all laugh and welcome him to come by for a discussion any time he wants. Abebe follows him to the front to ring in his purchase.

Lori and Pamoon get back to the boxes. After a few minutes, Lori says, "I liked very much when you talked about preaching your way to your people. Perhaps I should begin talking among my family and friends about how we are not the righteous ones of this land; that we all were immigrants at one time, and that we conveniently forget where we came from. Maybe if we all accept that, then we will understand others better. Abebe is right to be confused and feel lost.

"You know, once I heard one of my relatives say that if she gets sick she would never want an African doctor to treat her. It puzzled me how she could even say such a thing, and I was pleased when her sister told her that an African doctor probably has much more experience than a North American one. It seems she disagreed, as she continued to argue about it. These kinds of people are the ones who think they are better than anybody else or any other culture. They take everything for granted. But then here we are. As you said Pamoon, we all know what is wrong, but what do we do about it?"

"Ah my dear, we are so involved with our daily lives that we don't even know what is going on with our next door neighbour, not to mention how much we all unintentionally contribute to the misery of the people in other nations."

They continue working in thoughtful silence. Soon the three of them are busy with the routines of the day.

A few hours pass as the crew works nonstop: filling the shelves; attending to customers; cleaning the floor of the muddy messes tracked in by customers. From time to time they chat about another interesting topic, but are always interrupted by demanding customers.

The day is gone, and the street lights outside are turning on. It's raining hard, and the number of customers decreases. Lori's shift is over, but Abebe has made coffee, so she sits to talk some more, then says good night and leaves. As she closes the door behind her, she looks back into the store and smiles to see Pamoon and Abebe already beginning another of their hot political discussions. She walks away, whispering, "Such fine and intelligent people those two are."

She walks to her bus stop unable to wait to get home and hear about Tom's new job. Silence greets her as she opens the door, *"Oh, no welcome tonight. He must have fallen asleep,"* she thinks. She goes directly to her children's room, quietly opens the door and looks at their beautiful faces, covers them up, and puts a motherly kiss on each forehead. She then goes to her bedroom to find Tom is not there. She returns to her tiny living room, which is attached to the small kitchen, and sees Tom fast asleep on the sofa, waiting for her with a cold dinner on the table. "Oh, sweet; he prepared dinner for us."

She doesn't feel hungry, so she puts the food in the fridge. She takes her shoes and coat off and prepares to go to the bedroom, but with one look at Tom's face, she knows he will be chilly. She goes to the bedroom to bring out a warm blanket to cover Tom, then squeezes herself under it and into his arms. Tom moves around half awake, pulls her closer and holds her tight as the two of them sleep in a loving embrace right there.

After a while, Tom wakes up to shift his position, waking Lori too, "Ahh, I'm sorry I fell asleep. I was so tired."

"It's okay darling, I wanted to be with you too. Go to sleep now." Tom begins to caress her and touch her.

"No! No!" she says, with a kind but firm tone.

Tom pulls back a bit, and with a boyish tone mumbles, "Okay, okay."

Lori snuggles into him and apologizes for cutting things off. "I'm tired! I don't feel like having sex right now. We haven't been together for quite a while, and I do really want us to make love, but let's do it when the time is right, and the kids are not home."

"Tomorrow morning?" Tom says.

Lori jumps upright with a worried look, "What? What about tomorrow? Aren't you going to work? They laid you off already?"

"No, no, don't worry. They asked for a records check and they gave me a half-day off to get it done. I have to go take care of it early in the morning, and by the time I return the kids will be at school."

Still shaken, Lori settles herself back in his arms. They hold each other tight and soon fall asleep.

It is about 7:30 when the kids jump on them playfully. They rarely see Mom and Dad at home together because of their odd shifts. Tom and Lori wake up and wrestle with them for a bit. Then Tom jumps off the sofa as he remembers his appointment. He runs to the bathroom to wash up then get ready, and when he comes out Lori has two pieces of toast and a cup of coffee ready for him. He kisses her, takes his breakfast, and runs out. Lori helps her children get ready and decides to walk with them to school since she has no shift this morning. She loves this little luxury, which gives her a few minutes to be with her Joy and Jade. At the school yard, she kisses their cheeks and sends them in, watching as they disappear among the other students. She sighs and walks toward the grocery store. She's happy that she spent this time with them, though sad that this was the first time in several months. She is also happy that she doesn't have to work today, so she takes the opportunity to enjoy a leisurely walk.

At the store she buys what she needs for supper, though she's not pleased with the choices she must make, as the healthiest food is far too expensive. She remembers her daughter's stomach ache and the boy's toothache, and that the good doctor discouraged them all from eating chips or other processed foods. She wants to buy some grapes, but she knows that she doesn't have enough money. With a sigh she buys just enough grapes and two apples only for Joy and Jade.

She goes home where she prepares a lunch, all the while becoming worried as she wonders where Tom is. He finally arrives after twelve and runs to the bedroom to change as he apologizes for being late. "I'm so sorry my love, it was so busy there. I didn't know that many people would be there needing records checks. I had to stand in line for over an hour."

Lori comes to the bedroom and holds him tight, "That's okay. I am sorry for last night; was I mean to you?"

"No, no, you were right, it wasn't the time. I was so tired myself that I would have just embarrassed myself." Chuckling, they go to the kitchen to have a quick lunch. "We'll all have dinner together tonight and when the kids are sleeping we'll take care of each other." He then kisses her intimately and passionately.

He grabs his coat, and at the door says, "I mailed all your envelopes this morning."

"Which ones?"

"All those job applications and résumés that you prepared for those new postings last week."

"Ah, thank you darling! I forgot all about those yesterday."

After he has left, Lori sits on the sofa thinking cynically about those applications – how many the two of them have sent out over the past three years. Tom eventually did get a job, but not one as satisfying as he had before; and as for her, nothing yet. She worries and wonders if she can ever again employ her skills and training for a rewarding career. There is no question of going back to school because of the financial difficulties they already face.

She remembers when they were laid off and had to apply for employment insurance. Classes were set up for people accessing that service. In one of them the instructor indirectly hinted that only lazy people go on income assistance. She remembers how furious Tom was with that man for what he said.

Lori completes her housework and is preparing dinner when the kids arrive. She gives them snacks and instructs them to go to their room to do their homework. "I'll call you at five to set the table so we can have dinner together."

At that moment she realizes that she doesn't remember the last time they had all sat down to dinner as a family. She gets upset when she remembers how casually other parents at the school complained about such things, but only as a joke, as if it was simply customary to work like machines without having enough time for each other.

Tom arrives home, tired but happy. They sit around the table, having a wonderful dinner, talking about school, work and games.

Tom asks his kids if they have any new refugees in their school.

"Yes!" they both say at the same time, and then they blurt out together something about how the new children are not very happy, finishing off with, again at the same time, "Why?"

Lori and Tom are surprised to hear that the refugee children are unhappy, and surprised that both their children perceived the same thing. After a few moments of silence, Lori says, "Well, maybe they are frightened. When people are scared, they won't look happy. They do not know our language and they came from brutal war zones. Also, they may miss their friends and relatives."

Tom shakes his head and says, "We all really have to work together to put an end to all these wars, so that way people can live in their own communities where they grew up and have all their friends and family, and their memories."

The mood around the table changes. They eat the rest of their meal quietly. After dinner, Lori asks Tom to rest while the kids help her clean up the kitchen. She then goes to their room, plays with them a bit, reads a couple of stories, tucks them in and kisses them good night. She returns to her room to find Tom sleeping deeply. Smiling, she picks up the book Abebe gave her a week ago, begins to read.

She remembers her conversation with Abebe last week when she asked if it was true that many civil wars in Africa are due to ethnic and religious differences. As Lori holds the book, she recalls how Abebe was upset with her question, indicting her for blindly accepting the superficial analyses of the evening news. He told her that a little bit of research would reveal how Africa is at the post-colonial mercy of multinational corporations eager to profit from the resources there.

Lori looks at the book cover, "Wars and Conflict in Resource-Rich Countries." She remembers Pamoon trying to calm Abebe's agitation, holding him and telling him not to be too hard on Lori. She said Westerners often are unfamiliar with what immigrants know about the causes and effects of wars and exploitation.

Lori was embarrassed that she was unaware of what was really happening elsewhere, although she also noticed how Abebe's eyes shone when Pamoon held him.

She smiles at the memory, then reads the introduction of the book and the first chapter, seeing right away why Abebe asked her to read it. The book contains well-researched discussions about the long history of abuses in Africa, from the slave trade right through to today as people struggle with corruption and exploitations imposed by the dominant global economic system designed to favour the powerful and ignore local or sustainable communities. Any religious or ethnic tensions only help keep countries there weak and divided, making it easier to continue taking their valuable resources.

She continues to read through the second chapter, then on to the third. She just cannot stop reading. Lori has to go to work tomorrow and needs to sleep, but the material is so shocking to her that she cannot fall asleep. She has many questions for Abebe, and now understands why he became angry that day, as she herself is feeling that same anger right now. Part of that feeling comes from realizing how people's day-to-day priorities keep them from finding time to read and educate themselves on these issues.

Again she realizes she must get some sleep, so she tiptoes to her bag to put the book inside it to read on the bus tomorrow. She chuckles when she thinks how she might become like Abebe, reading anywhere she has an opportunity. She figures that can only be a good thing considering how knowledgeable he is. "I would be happy to be like him," Lori whispers to herself. "Pamoon appreciates him, and I do too." She tiptoes quietly to bed, as she has no intention of waking Tom up. She wants to fall asleep contemplating her newly acquired knowledge. She cannot wait to share her new insights about the oppressed regions of the world later on with Tom.

Alsoomse: Independent

Aponi: Butterfly

Sokanon: Rain

ALSOOMSE

The road looks dark and daunting. *"It must be about five o'clock,'* she thinks. She is trying to walk as far as possible away from her little town so that she can reach the main road before daylight. It is early morning, and chilly. She wraps herself in her thin jacket and walks faster to warm up. She looks back and sees the faint lights of her little hometown. She has tears in her eyes, but she knows that she has to leave. As soon as she passes the corner she cannot see the town anymore, so she steps back to have one last look at her birth place, where the people she loves so much are still sleeping. She smiles as she imagines them lying warm under their covers, then continues on resolutely knowing she has a long way ahead of her and goals to achieve. She starts to run towards the main road hoping she won't see anyone from her town there.

Near the road, she sits on a rock and anytime a car approaches she gets up to look at the driver. If it is an old man or a woman she puts her thumb out for a ride, but nobody is willing to stop for her.

It is now about eleven o'clock. She is tired, hungry and thirsty – but cautious and aware of her surroundings. Her hands hold pepper spray tightly in one pocket and the soft handle of a little knife in the other. It's not a killing knife, but it is good enough as a distraction and for creating an opportunity to run away if she has to.

Eventually a car pulls aside. She releases the knife and holds the pepper spray tightly as she approaches the vehicle. The driver is a middle-aged woman, who asks with a kind smile, "Where are you going?" she asks.

"Vancouver."

"OK. Get in, that's where I am headed."

She slips her backpack off her shoulder as she gets into the car, setting the pack between her feet; though she quickly puts her hand back into her pocket to grip the knife.

"Could you please put your seatbelt on?"

"Oh, sure."

She snaps the seatbelt in and then once more returns her hand to her pocket. The woman glances at her, pulls the car onto the road, and then asks her name.

"Alsoomse."

"Hmm, you're Cree, right? And your name means Independent?"

"I think so. How do you know?"

"I am Cree too, but from Ontario. My name is Aponi."

"But you don't look like me; you look like white people."

"Yes, and I was raised with them too."

"What? You said you were Cree. Why were you brought up with white people then? Sorry, I hope you don't mind me asking?"

"No, I don't mind. We have a few hours to drive, we may as well talk." She smiles at her and continues. "Well, I do not know who my father is and my mother is half-native. My mother's family were Native American from a reservation south of the border. I am sure you have read or heard about what was happening in those days on those reservations. My grandmother ran off to Canada with my mother, who was only three at the time, thinking life might be better there. They settled with the Cree in northern Ontario and started a new life. My grandmother met a good Cree man, married, and had a few more children, but my mother was my grandfather's favourite. He knew she had had a tough life.

"Soon Canada's residential school system scooped up local children and took them away from their homes. That included my mother. She was raped there and had me at the age of fifteen. When the sisters found out she was pregnant, they called her all kinds of names, as they were sure she had been naughty with one of the boys in the school. But then I was born as white as you see now. They took me away from her and gave me to a white family for adoption. They called me Lisa."

"O my, that is brutal... did they hit you or call you names too?"

"No, no, I have to be honest, they were nice and polite."

Alsoomse laughs hard, finding herself relaxing, letting go of her knife. "What do you mean they were nice and polite?"

"Well, they were rather respectful with one another, but did not know how to show affection. They didn't seem to know how to love and care for each other.

Everything was a routine, and naturally they were the same with me: simply nice and polite."

Alsoomse looks at Aponi with a smile, "Well, instead of that, I'll just say that you are kind and friendly."

"Ha! Thanks for that. How about you? Why you are going to Vancouver?"

"I have been accepted into nursing school, and I am headed off to start my program!"

"What? Wasn't there anyone in your family who could drive you there for such a wonderful occasion?"

"My mother does have a car, but she doesn't want me to go. We had a fight last night – again – and I left home sulking. I went to my aunt's house where I had all my belongings hidden in my cousin's room. Before dawn I left the house."

"Ah, you are running away from home."

"No, I am going to school."

Aponi looks at her sadly, with a kind smile. "Well, make sure you visit home when you get your first report card so that your mother can see that you are in the city only to study, and doing great as well."

"Oh, she doesn't need that," Alsoomse says. "I graduated as an honour student; top of my class! And not just in grade twelve; all through school. She just fears the city and doesn't want me to go away. Our little town has no college, so I had to leave."

Aponi glances over at her a few more times, then says, "Well sweetheart, we have a few more hours to drive, and now it's your turn to tell me about yourself and your family. Why does your mother fear the city so?"

Alsoomse looks at her with smile. "OK, sure." She reaches into her backpack to bring out her water bottle, has a sip and says, "I have two brothers. The older one is smart and studies at U Vic, but of course he's not as smart as I am." The two laugh.

"Oh, so your mother has no fear for your brother?"

"Sure she does, and they fought too. She didn't want him go either. Then my uncle found a job in Victoria and my brother moved in with him. My younger brother is in elementary school."

They are quiet for some time. Alsoomse looks out the window admiring the colourful autumn trees, enjoying the beautiful season.

Aponi sighs. "I do not understand your mother's fear."

Alsoomse says, "Well, she had a tough life; her own mother went to residential school just like yours. After leaving that place she became an alcoholic and died when my mother was very young. My mother thinks cities are dangerous for us, full of the same people that put us in residential schools. She strongly believes that we have to live together and grow stronger as a community."

"Don't you like to be in your community?"

"Of course I like to be there. But I also want to educate myself and then return to my community to help improve it. Anytime we went to Vancouver, I felt as if I was travelling to another country. Our little town is so small and underdeveloped. Our drinking water makes everyone sick and our little clinic looks like something in a third world country. Are we not in the same country as Vancouver? How is that, can you tell me?" She folds her arms and looks sad and confused. "My mother says she needs time to heal and doesn't want to leave."

They approach a rest stop where Aponi asks if she would like to have a bite to eat. Alsoomse agrees so they stop for some coffee and sandwiches. They bring their food to a table and eat quietly. Aponi looks at her from time to time sadly, not knowing what to say to this young, smart, beautiful and ambitious girl. She knows the young lady is right about how there are many reserves that are run down and have poor drinking water and other issues. And yes, people also need to heal, yet at the same time for how long?

Aponi's thoughts are making her face gloomy, and Alsoomse says, "Did I say something wrong? You look unhappy."

"Oh, no, no, you didn't say anything wrong; as a matter of fact I am so happy to have met such a smart and determined young lady. At the same time I feel for your mother. Many of our people believe the system is still out to get us, to somehow eliminate us. They don't even know who's out to get them or how. But as you said, the quality of life in our communities is in such a desperate state that people there don't trust or believe in anybody but themselves and their own people. And those communities are so poor."

"Well, yes, and that's why I want to leave and take advantage of the programs out there; I want to educate myself, to bring my skills back to my community. When we sit there and try to heal, nothing changes. But if we educate ourselves, learn from the past and demand our rights, we can heal much faster, because we will be seeing transformations along the way. But my mother's fears won't let us move on, it seems."

Aponi nods her head, then looks at her watch, gets up, and says, "OK let's go." As they pull out onto the highway once again, Aponi asks Alsoomse if she has a place to stay. "Oh yes, through my registration I have applied for a dormitory, so I am all set." After a pause she says, "You see how many immigrants and white people are in all the colleges and universities. Why not us? If we do not use what is ours, it is our fault. I didn't have any trouble getting accepted when I sent in my application. I have a right to be there too, and study what I want. And be who I want to be."

She is tired and angry, and Aponi reaches over to caress her beautiful, long and thick black hair. "I am so proud of you. And I am sure your mother will come around as well. You set up your program all by yourself. You are determined to go to school and have a skill. Oh girl, you are a dream for any mother. I'm sure your mother loves and appreciates you. That's why she is so afraid that something might happen to such a wonderful kid as you."

Alsoomse sighs, "If she could only trust me; I would not go out with anyone bad and naughty. I just want to study and make a difference. That is how I'll heal: by showing who I am; by showing that I'm not the stereotype they have about our people."

They sit quietly as Aponi drives and soon Alsoomse falls asleep.

Eventually they get to Vancouver, but Alsoomse does not wake up. She looks like she needs the sleep, so Aponi stops the car to sit quietly for some time, until eventually the young woman wakes and looks around.

"Ah, we are here."

"You didn't tell me where your dorm is, so I had to wait for you to wake up and guide me."

Alsoomse smiles and reaches into her backpack pocket to take out the address to give it to Aponi. She looks at it and says they are not far. As she resumes driving, Aponi wishes Alsoomse all the best in her studies.

"Thanks so much, I'm really looking forward to it. And thank you for driving me here. Could I contribute some money for your gas?"

"Ah, no darling, you just promise to do as you said. And in a few days call your mother and let her know where you are. What is her name by the way?"

"Sokanon!"

"How beautiful; Vancouver's weather. Hah!"

"Yes, her name means 'Rain'. It's a beautiful name and I miss her already. I will call her in a few days, for sure! Would you like to come and meet her?"

"Oh, I would! I would love to meet the wonderful woman who raised you: a truly independent, strong young lady such as you. I would love to meet her. Ah, we're here now. Let me give you my number. Make sure you call me!"

They exchange numbers. Aponi is happy that she knows where Alsoomse lives and that she is safe enough. They hug and say farewell then go their separate ways.

Aponi stops the car just around the corner and waits a bit to make sure Alsoomse gets into her building. She is so pleased to have met her and is so proud of her. She thinks: *"I will make sure she has everything she needs, and that will be my own healing to help our young, motivated girl along her way."*

With a happy smile of satisfaction, she drives away.

Aillard: Noble strength

Aglaia: Beauty, splendour

TINY

Sun shines like a bent arrow through the thick waterfall and a beautiful rainbow appears in the powdery mist filling the air. The falls splash into the pond below, scattering across the surrounding rocks and leaves leaving them wet and shining. The rainbow hovers over the deep pool, enhancing the fresh sparkling feel of the space as the water tumbles onward toward the river.

It is a magnificent, peaceful and beautiful scene far from the madness of the city. She listens carefully, enjoying all the sounds: lively birds darting among the surrounding trees; a breeze caressing leaves into a delicate whispering dance; and of course the reverberating undertone of the waterfall, which sometimes overwhelms the delicate purity of the other musical songs of nature.

She is wet and cold, but doesn't move as she sits on a rock just above the falls, looking down at the river moving through the valley. She contemplates how nice it might be to live in this forest permanently, near this reliable river, far from the treacherous town. She whispers to herself, "Perhaps I could have the peace I need right here. But if he doesn't join me, I surely would miss him."

She gets up to look around, and choose one of the paths down through the trees. After about fifteen minutes she can scarcely hear the waterfall in the distance. *"This is better, I can hear the sounds of the forest more clearly here,"* she thinks as she walks toward her little cottage surrounded by tall trees in the heart of the woods. She notices smoke coming out of her chimney. "Ah, he's here. I have missed him so."

She arrives at her door, but before she can go in, her big hairy friend jumps on her in a joyful greeting. They play happily, rolling around in the leaves on the ground. She then gets up, brushes herself off, and settles into her friend's big hairy arms. She talks to her, and the bear makes some noises as if she is responding. The cottage door opens and Aillard comes out smiling, "Before I can get a hug, she is always there to greet you first."

She gets up laughing with joy. They hug each other tightly for a few minutes. He kisses her passionately, and then whispers, "It's so difficult without you. Please come home Aglaia, please."

"No, no, we've talked about this; you come here. I'm settling in quite well. This year I will have my own home-grown food, which means I will come less frequently into the city. Please, you come here to join us."

Aillard kisses her forehead, and goes back inside frowning. She looks at him for a bit, then gets back to Tiny, wrestling with her a bit more. The bear stands on her hind legs, and together they walk hand-in-hand to a shed not far from her cottage.

Aglaia opens the door and they go inside the dim, cool space. She picks out a pretty bag that she hand-crafted herself, which contains a few fish she cut up yesterday for Tiny. She offers some to her, but the bear refuses. Aglaia looks surprised, "What's wrong? You always eat from my hand!"

She strokes Tiny some more and kisses the tip of her nose, but the bear still refuses to eat. So, Aglaia puts the fish back in the bag and tosses it on the bench for another day, but then Tiny suddenly grabs the bag with her mouth, turns, and runs off into the woods. Aglaia stands dumbfounded, trying to understand what just happened.

"I saw her with a big male bear this morning," Aillard says, walking up to the shed's door with a grin. "She has found her mate, so Tiny lives better than I do."

She walks toward him smiling, "Are you serious?"

"When I arrived, she was playing intimately with the other bear, who wanted to attack me. Tiny kept him back, then greeted me as she usually does while the other bear watched. The male left, but I'm sure Tiny took the fish for her partner."

"Ah, how beautiful! Perhaps this winter she will have cubs. I'll have to clean the underground room for her den. Also, I'll have to make sure that Tiny and her cubs have food when she comes out of hibernation."

Aglaia walks toward her cottage muttering plans to herself, but Aillard takes her arm, gently pulling her to his chest. He holds her tight, smells her hair, and kisses her passionately on her cheeks, forehead, and on her lips. She pulls back and looks into his sad eyes, "I'm sorry, I am so sorry. I know I have abandoned you, forgive me. But you know I cannot live in the city anymore. I cannot watch the world as it is and continue living the superficial life fashioned for us. Join me; we can be happy here.

"We cannot win. Without the collaboration of people of understanding, we cannot change anything, and I'm tired of trying. Over seven billion people live on this planet, with probably six billion of them being walking zombies, doing nothing but eating, drinking, fornicating and plotting get-rich-quick schemes, quite unaware of how responsible they all are for the world's daily miseries. I do not want to be part of that crowd. I am happy here where my only problem is missing you." She takes him by the arm for the walk back to her cottage.

"Not enough," he says.

"What do you mean 'not enough'; you know I love you very much!"

"Not so much that you will live with me. You have left me, our home, and our life together to live in the middle of nowhere. We see each other every couple of weeks, and when you are out here alone, I am so worried that I cannot sleep and I'm distracted at work."

"Ah, don't start again! Whenever you come here we fight and you leave in a sulk. This is my home now. If you want to argue this way every time, then why do you come at all?"

She goes to take a shower, slamming the door angrily. Aillard looks sorrowfully at that closed bathroom door, then walks to the kitchen to attend to the food he was making before she returned from her walk. The rooms are all tidy with everything in its place, though by contrast, books and papers are scattered all around her laptop. He goes to her desk and notices one neat stack of papers with a title on the first page.

"Oh, it seems she has completed her new book," as he begins to read. Aillard slowly settles into the chair beside her desk, becoming absorbed in the narrative, and doesn't even notice when Aglaia quietly enters the room drying her hair. She sees him reading. She quietly comes up behind him, kisses his hair, and holds his shoulder. "What do you think?"

"So far looks great! I'm not done yet. A novelette, hey?"

"Yes, when I got to that last page I thought it seemed good enough, and I'm happy with that ending. Mmm, your food smells delicious. I'm hungry; let's go eat. Then, while I'm napping, you can read the rest. I did not sleep enough last night."

"I don't sleep well either, worrying about you here alone."

"Why are you worried about me? I sleep with a big, strong bear lying beside my bed. Who can come near me? She will rip any intruder apart. You're not worried about Tiny being with me in the same room, are you?"

"Oh no, I'm not concerned about her at all. Rather, I'm worried about the two-footed animals. I'm afraid someone could find you out here alone, and hurt both of you."

"Well, I sometimes worry about that too. But it was in the city that we lost our child. In the city they hurt me, and with the way the laws are set up, our system did not, nor could not, do anything about it."

"I know, I know. Okay, let's go eat. What was wrong last night? Why did you not sleep well?" he asks as he holds her hand while they walk to the kitchen.

"Well, first there was the howling wind, then I thought I heard something, so I got my gun and looked outside but nobody was there. Well, I couldn't sleep after that."

"Ah, see what I mean? Come on Aglaia, please come home. I have found a beautiful house near the ocean; it's far enough from the city, while at the same time near enough for me to drive home in little over an hour, and come to you every evening. Please at least come to see it."

"No! What about Tiny? We cannot leave her here nor bring her close to the city. Our fault for making her dependent on us, but that's how it is and now I am her mother. Also, I know you could work from here. You could go into the city weekly or monthly if you want. You can drive there from here in a little over three hours."

She takes a deep breath, looking at him angrily. "With the waterfall on our land we are producing our own electricity, and your tower up on the hill gives you your connection to the city. Why did you put that tall ugly tower up there if you did not want to stay and work from here? Why? Why don't you come here and go in to the office whenever you need to? Do you miss the city more than me? It's possible to live here, so why don't you?"

He says nothing as he pours more wine for her. For a time they sit quietly eating their meal. She looks at him thinking, *"He is so stubborn! Ah, how I have missed him; if only he would stay here."* She smiles. After finishing her meal she gets up and sits on his lap.

"Thanks, that was delicious," she says, kissing him on his cheek, biting softly on his ear.

"Anything for you, my love." He kisses her neck, then her lips, and then he picks her up and takes her to the bedroom. They lie down in each other's arms. He caresses and kisses her as she gradually falls asleep. After a few minutes, he carefully moves away, covers her up, and goes to the kitchen to clean up and contemplate their situation.

Aillard then returns to the living room where he picks up her new book. Making himself comfortable in the armchair, he continues reading. The story begins in New York City where they met at the Museum of Natural History. It continues with how they fell in love, and then describes their travel adventures, their years in college, and how they moved on to begin their careers and start their future together. He reads of all the beautiful memories they shared. How happy they were when they learned about the pregnancy, and the fun they had designing the best room in their house for their child.

Then his tears run down his face as he reads about the driver that ran her down and killed the baby before he was even born, about the injuries Aglaia sustained that ensured they could never have a child again. He reads on as the story describes how the driver was a repeat hit-and-run offender. How weak laws and high-priced lawyers ensured that the man served only minimal time in jail and was soon free again, having basically gotten away with murder.

He rests the book on his lap, trying to keep quiet as his tears run down his face and onto his shirt. Aillard can understand why Aglaia would rather be alone in the middle of a forest than live in the city. He begins to question why he is worried about her here. *"Wasn't it in the city that we lost our child, and lost any chance to have another? No, perhaps she really is safer here. Also, I can see her writing has improved greatly since she moved out here. Maybe I should try to see what I can do to join her."* He shakes his head and continues reading. "She is good," he whispers.

Time passes and he completes the book. He sits in thought for a while, waiting for Aglaia to wake up, but then he joins her in the bedroom and quietly slips under the blanket. He soon falls asleep too.

The cottage is dark, and the bear walks anxiously around the house looking in through the windows. She moans for her mother and bangs at the door. Every morning, Tiny goes on her adventurous day trips into the forest, though never too far from home. She explores the forest and eats berries, and she now has a mate and companion to play with. In the evening she returns to her mom, Aglaia.

Tiny was only a few days old when Aglaia found her. The mother had been shot before she was even born. They think the wounded mother bear must have made it to her den, given birth to her two cubs, then died of her wounds. One of the cubs died too, and Aillard and Aglaia found the other one, so small, hungry and fragile. They called her Tiny. She became their child. Aglaia bottle-fed her, then hand-fed her, and gave her baths every night just like a baby. For over a year Tiny slept in the bed with them, but as she got bigger and heavier, nobody was comfortable with that situation anymore. They made up a place for her right beside their bed so that Aglaia could reach down to comfort Tiny any time she needed. Caring for the cub meant that Aglaia spent almost all her time at their cottage.

Tiny is about three years old now, and Aglaia has lived there with the bear the whole time. Aillard is not happy because he is now usually alone in the city. Though he comes for visits, mostly weekly, when he is very busy the visits become biweekly and that is the time he becomes worried and quite unhappy. However, he cannot convince his love to come back to the city, back to the life they had before that accident. Three years have gone by like this because the bear is utterly domesticated and they cannot leave her alone in the forest, partly because she is unafraid of the very humans that killed her mother. As a child loves her mother, so Tiny loves Aglaia. She is loyal to her mother and very protective of her. As bizarre as it looks, they are a functioning family with unconditional love and affection for one another.

But now, Tiny is upset, banging harder at the door, finally waking Aglaia who runs to open it up. Tiny growls her distress, then steps back, as she has been trained, to wait for a cleanup before she steps into the house. Aglaia begins to wash her and Aillard fetches the huge towels they use to dry her off, but he suddenly realizes that the water running off the bear is pink. He runs over and starts exploring her body, and Tiny screams when Aillard touches her right arm.

"She's hurt," he says.

They quickly finish the cleaning, dry her down, and bring her inside so they can examine her arm. Sure enough they find a big cut there, so they clean it, carefully shave the hair around it, then bind the wound. All the while, Tiny patiently and trustfully watches them attend to her so kindly.

"What do you think, did someone do this to her, or did she cut it on a branch or something?" asks Aglaia.

"Mm, I don't think this was an accident. This was done by a knife."

"Ah, and you want me to leave her here and come to the city? She must have gotten too close to someone who doesn't know her. We did not plan to domesticate her. You see? Her life will be in danger here without us."

Aillard holds Aglaia affectionately, "I know, I know, you're right. I will join you two and go into the city when I must. I do love it when I'm here. After all, I found this wonderful area for us and built this home here. I love it as much as you do. We just have to make sure we have things properly set for our expenses, okay? As soon as I secure that, we will live here for good."

Aglaia's eyes light up as she squeezes him tight and kisses him all over, saying how much she loves and misses him when he is not here with them. "I'm sure we are secure. We'll sell our house in the city which can pay to fence the entire area; what is it, sixty acres? And with the rest of the money we will add to this cottage and make it bigger and homier. With my garden we can have all the fruits and vegetables we need for the whole year, and we can go into town for any other necessities. We can do it, I am sure, because you won't have to quit your work what with that damn ugly tower on the hill connecting you to the world. My writing can earn a little money; yes, I'm sure we can manage our expenses. Please begin to work on it; promise me?"

He holds her tight, whispering in her ear, "I promise you."

They stay in each other's arms for a few more minutes, then turn back to poor Tiny who has been patiently watching their excited chatter, waiting for them to get back to tending her wound. Aillard works on Tiny's arm while Aglaia soothes her, the bear responding with special sounds as if they are conversing back and forth.

When they are done, Aillard goes to the kitchen to put the kettle on for tea, thinking, *"Oh boy, I have promised, and now I'll need to work on transferring my workplace here. How is that going to work out? Ah, is it really possible?'* He smiles as he works around the kitchen, *"Well, there's only one way to find out, and that's by beginning the process and seeing if being one with nature away from city can coexist with a career that provides for my wife and our hairy fairy forest child."*

He laughs at his sentiments and joins his family in the living room to find his wife leaning on Tiny's belly with the big bear's arms wrapped around her delicate guardian. He has always been somewhat nervous seeing this level of intimacy, fearing that Tiny may crush Aglaia in some moment of unawareness. But he says nothing and sits beside them. The bear rolls away from Aglaia and playfully body-checks Aillard into some wrestling. So Aglaia gets up and goes to her desk. "Oh, I see you have finished reading the book. Did you like it?"

"You wrote beautifully, as always. It's sad because it's about our life's tragedy, but I actually loved the part criticizing the law and urging effective changes in regards to deadly car accidents at the hands of careless drivers. You pointed out flawlessly that laws need to be implemented to make sure people care about how they operate a vehicle, and that there will be severe consequences for negligent driving, especially for drivers who already have bad records. Yes, that was all good, but it comes back to our loss, which is distressing."

He looks at her with tearful eyes, sighing. "Anyway, in general, I love the way you play with life stories, and highlight people's responsibilities towards one another. I especially like your games with words and names. I love it all!"

She smiles and thanks him for his usual support, "You know, my next tale will be Tiny's life story: where we found her; how we raised her. And I am sure we will soon be grandparents, so please begin fencing all around our lands, as I do not want people coming in and attacking them, or the government coming and taking them. We will provide for them here, and make sure these bears and people have nothing to do with one another."

Aillard ponders as he pours the tea, *"Oh boy, the government. Did I think about that? I have to make sure these premises are secured. I am sure someone cut Tiny. Yes, after today I must get to the fencing before anything else."*

He comes out of the kitchen to find Tiny laying down on the floor at the sofa, where Aglaia sits reading while rubbing Tiny's back with her feet. He sets the tea on the table, then sits beside his love and holds her. Tiny looks up at their embrace with annoyance and gets up to push herself between the two of them. They both laugh out loud at Tiny's competitive behaviour and jealousy for her mom's attention. She settles down between them resting her head on Aglaia's chest, licking her neck from time to time and making low growling sounds as her two parents continue laughing.

REFUGEES

We sit with a group of reporters, nurses and volunteers on the cold beach, waiting for yet another boat to arrive. There were fatalities in the previous one; five people fell into the water and disappeared.

We discuss who is helping more in this situation, ordinary people or European government officials. The discussion is passionate, and there is disagreement on both sides. However, we all do agree that if there were no wars, all these people would surely rather live in their own homelands than risk such a dangerous journey.

It's getting dark and cold, though the moon shines beautifully. Then Josh shouts out, "a boat!" We all look in the direction he is pointing, out in the Mediterranean Sea where we can see a vessel approaching.

As it gets closer, we can easily see the occupants huddling close to each other for warmth against the freezing ocean breeze. The bright moon regales their gloomy night, giving them hope; but the shabby boat slides up and then down the rough waves in a slow, never-ending rhythm of fear.

They arrive at the shore and stare fearfully at us. The boat seems to be holding many more people than its capacity. As we rush into the water to help them, I see a very agitated little girl, about five years old, crying nonstop. An angry man is shouting something, and we call for a translator who explains that the child's mother fell into the water before her eyes, and then her father jumped in to save her, but both disappeared into the cold, dark water. They searched for some time, but couldn't find them, and with great anguish they had to continue to shore.

I gather some courage and go to the little girl to try to calm her, but she is inconsolable. So, I hold her tightly in my arms, though she cries and fights me, until eventually she calms enough to gaze spellbound into my alien face, and then slump slowly into an exhausted sleep.

We guide the group over to the prepared shelters. I carry the girl myself to a little bed and sit beside her as she slumbers. She seems to be dreaming, as she is so agitated and mumbles something from time to time, or cries out. I wonder what I should do tomorrow when this weary little angel wakes up. How am I to answer her when she asks for her parents? How am I going to succour this shattered soul? How many like her are all around here needing comfort?

Many days pass, and many more vessels arrive on this and other foreign beaches, carrying desperate hopes for a brighter future. They are handed pieces of bread and water, and then stored in dirty camps. Nobody wants them.

The shining moon still entertains, but are they any safer? Is there really any hope?

WILL

He strolls in his favourite park, feeding the ducks, even though he knows he is not supposed to. He sits on the bench that has his memorial plaque; it's inscribed with a beautiful Robert Frost poem for his love. For a long while after she passed he was not able to sit here.

He thinks of her last days and how difficult it was for her with all that pain, although remembering their forty beautiful years of life together helps to counter his sadness. They had never disagreed on anything, and friends and family envied their life together.

He lingers in the park a while longer, then walks to the pharmacy to pick up his package.

He arrives home and goes directly to the kitchen to make himself a cocktail. He returns to his room, drinks heartily, and begins to look back on his life as he lays down on his bed. He soon feels cold but has no energy to get up, so he pulls the cover over himself and smiles grimly, *"It will be even colder soon."*

He opens his eyes, and feels tightness around his wrist. He realizes they have found him. He takes a deep breath, *"Do they think that they have rescued me? A man of my age and discernment; can one not decide even then? They must have read my note. That is my will!"*

He closes his eyes, sighing, "What right do they have to judge, and tie me to a bed? My fault, I did not plan well. With my next shot at it, I will ensure there is no return – and no note."

MY SUMMER VACATION

Ever since high school where I learned about Egyptian history and the pyramids, I have wanted to visit that country to see its amazing monuments. Although I grew up into a busy life like everyone else, I never forgot my dream. For years I saved up for my trip, planning to visit the Pyramids of Djoser and western Giza, as well as the Great Sphinx.

Finally, the time came. Excited, I called my Egyptian friend Nefertiti to ask if she wanted to go with me and my partner Alphonso, both as a friend and a tour guide.

"Carina, this is not a sensible idea," she said. "A trip to the Middle East is too dangerous these days." Well, I could see her point, but I was willing to take the risk. "Why Egypt?" she continued. "Why don't you go to the

Caribbean, or somewhere around here, and have fun in the sun by the ocean?"

I was surprised. "Why do you say that? You know how much I love to explore our world's cultures. Egypt has one of the most interesting histories on this planet!"

"Sure, I understand, but you should be aware that they are tired of tourists there, Carina. You watch the news and follow world affairs closely, don't you? You can see how so much of the Middle East is afflicted with wars and conflict of some sort. People there see us as the cause of many of their problems, and hate it when we show up with our carefree attitude as if nothing is wrong. Blowing up tourist buses is just one symptom of that."

I had never thought of it that way! We privileged people in the Western world are living in heaven, while others are having a tough time, often because of our actions. Nevertheless, I asked Nefertiti, "Isn't it true that tourism is good for their economies?"

"They are past that justification dear Carina, and they just do not like tourists anymore."

I could see my wise friend's point. We discussed world affairs for a while longer, agreeing on how easy we have it here compared to much of the world.

I waited for Alphonso to return home, and with one look at my face he asked, "What's wrong, my love?"

I told him about my talk with Nefertiti, so we deliberated on it and decided to postpone the overseas trip to a later time; we chose to wait and see if the future ever offers this planet peace for all. We agreed that we had to reflect more on how much we as individuals have to do with the madness overseas. So we planned a nice vacation that year in our little cottage near the city. We always enjoyed our stays there anyway.

When the time came, we left early in the morning, heading out of the city for the beautiful drive along the coast. We soon came to one of my favourite places, a magnificent waterfall surrounded by a peaceful and beautiful forest, far from the madness of the city. We sat there for some time, not wishing to move even though it was cold. Sitting on a rock just above the falls, looking down at the river moving through the valley, I contemplated how nice it might be to reside in this forest permanently, near this rushing river and far from the bustling town.

"Why don't we live at our cottage?" I said as we walked back to our car. "Perhaps we could have the peace we need right here. You can work from home, which I am already doing myself." It wasn't the first time I had lobbied for moving out to the country, and I could see Alphonso was thinking about what I said positively.

We drove quietly for the last stretch, soon arriving at our cottage. While Alphonso unpacked our supplies from the car, I walked into the woods to try to hear the waterfall in the distance. *This is nice too. I can hear the sounds of the forest better here.*" I walked back through the tall trees toward our little cottage surrounded by the woods. I brought in the last bag and found Alphonso sitting on the sofa staring into the distance. "So, what do you think?" I asked.

"Well," he said, "I think it is doable. I know how much you want to get away from city, and I also know your writing is much better out here. You seem much more relaxed away from urban distractions. You know that I enjoy your writing on the critical issues of our world's disastrous wars and displacements, and your thoughts and furies flourish much better in this place!"

"Sure, but what is the point? People don't seem to care about others anymore."

"Yes, some do. Maybe not as many as you would wish, but some do."

I turned to the window and looked out on the pleasant scene. "Okay then. So, this year on our vacation, I will write about Egypt and her unresolved revolution, about why there is an anti-tourist mood there now, and the role Western societies play in the troubles there."

"Ah, that's my girl! Go for it! That's an important thing to write about, even if only one person reads it. You writers have a mission. That is to foster awareness in any way you can. You should keep writing more! Promise me you will and I promise to begin working on transferring ourselves out here."

I stared at him, delighted; unsure if I had heard correctly. I had been nagging Alphonso about this for over a year, and now did he just agree? Well, in all those wonderful days on our vacation, all I remember is his promise that we would soon be moving there for good; that, and my promise to him that I would write more about my passionate desire for a war-free world.

RACISM? SEXISM? OR SIMPLY LACK OF ACCOUNTABILITY?

Once upon a time, not very long ago in a few divisions of our public sector, a new federal program was implemented which was designed to aid newly arriving immigrants with integration into public organizations, and into the larger Canadian society in general. This new program was set up in several provinces. In one organization, the administration worked on assembling a team of people to carry out the duties required in this new program. As was usual, these positions were announced internally first, and if appropriate applicants from within could not be found, ads were placed with outside agencies. From within the division, a skilled and hard-working woman from the Middle East applied for the position - let's call her Rose. Rose had strong experience in that field and was well qualified for the credentials requested, so she had no problem being hired for one of the positions.

Rose loved the new program because she would be helping newly arrived immigrants through challenges with which she herself was personally familiar. Rose had already been in Canada for over two decades, but she remembered how it felt to be alone in a new land, not knowing the language or the culture, and dealing with the stress of leaving behind loved ones to start all over again with no support. She knew very well how it feels to be detached and separated from everything one knows, and how difficult it is to get used to a new home and fit in with a new culture. It was well known in the organization that she would be passionate about the job and would perform superbly.

One of the required qualifications to join the new team was fluency in one of the key languages. As we all know, ethnic groups tend to congregate. In this team's area, there were heavy concentrations of people from three countries: the Middle Eastern one that Rose was from, a particular Far Eastern one, and China. The first two groups were by far the biggest in population, so management was especially looking for people who were fluent in English and those two languages, plus Chinese, thus allowing the team to communicate between the newcomers and division staff, and more importantly allowing for understanding the problems of clients based on direct knowledge of the language and culture. Three people were hired, each with fluency in one of the three major languages. An outside multi-cultural agency was retained for translation services with the few clients encountered from any other language group.

The program was designed to help integrate newcomers and their families, helping them to adjust to their new environment and new culture so that they could focus as much as possible on learning and thriving, becoming productive citizens and partners within society at large. Efforts were implemented in assisting with understanding Canadian culture and the education system, as well as where to go to resolve any problems. These included workshops, counselling, group activities, and systematic outreach. Rose looked forward to working in such a wonderful program.

Rose began by increasing her knowledge about it; researching and learning about the successes of a similar program that had been operating effectively in another province over the past couple of years, thus inspiring its expansion into more provinces that had concentrations of new immigrants.

A week before the program began, the three team members were sent for orientation and a full week's training. There Rose met her two co-workers. One was a sweet Chinese lady and the other was an Eastern European man whom she recognized. Rose was quite surprised to see him as she knew he couldn't possibly have the language skill requirement for the Far Eastern community he was representing, so she asked him why he was there.

He smiled and responded, "Flexibility!"

Rose was quite concerned with this and didn't know what to do. It turns out that this man was someone she knew from a previous job, and knew well enough to know that he had no language credentials for this position, nor the requisite experience or education. Over the preceding years, she had told a close friend about a co-worker in a group home where she had worked. People there had come to dub this co-worker "Disgrace to the Human Race" because of his irresponsible and negligent behaviours. When Rose left that job she thought she was free of him, and now was devastated to find that she would have to work with him again, particularly in such a sensitive job.

Rose recalled how, at that group home for autistic children, he would frequently be late, or disappear mid-shift with vague excuses, or break protocol with the children for his own ends. Rather than having any professional concern for the children, he seemed to be chiefly interested in befriending management in order to help cover his failings, and with flirting up any female co-workers who would tolerate his advances. Those who wouldn't put up with his attentions found that complaining to management was of no use, as managers had already been sweet-talked into his camp. He made no secret of having affairs with married women, and Rose just found him to be an all-round repellent person. Co-workers soon learned to distrust him: one day he would be so late that the shift before him would have to stay overtime; another day he would take quiet kids to the theatre and leave a female worker alone to sustain injuries while trying to handle a violent child.

It was no surprise to Rose that this man had lost his job at that group home. Now she was worried that his stated desire for "flexible hours" meant that he was merely looking for another opportunity to do what he pleased. Apparently, he had somehow convinced the management of this new program that he was qualified for the position, including the required fluency in a language he did not actually know. But how had he done that? It seemed odd that management had not tested his comprehension of a language that it seemed likely he did not know, even though the contract specifically required fluency in one the three major minority languages. This was not the first time Rose had encountered failings in management processes, and she would not find management personnel any better at admitting or correcting their mistakes in this case either. At present, it just sent shivers down her back thinking that she had to now work with this particularly unscrupulous man again.

Once the training week was over, the team got to work contacting newly-immigrated clients to render assistance where needed. One of the key elements in the team's strategy was to develop and present workshops on various relevant themes so that large groups could be provided with helpful information all at once. The two ladies soon settled into their routine, however they couldn't help but notice that their co-worker -- let's call him Boris -- seemed to be mostly missing in action. He would arrive at 9 am, or maybe 10, or maybe 11, put in some time at his computer, then perhaps announce that he was off to the "library" to do some research for the rest of the day. No interviews with clients; no workshops. The team's supervisor would always find that Boris was said to be "on site" at some divisional location, or helping a client to access resources.

Because site managers had been advised that his main role in the new program was to support the large Far Eastern community in our region, they soon became aware that Boris didn't know the language when he was called in to facilitate communication with a family. The program was new, so busy managers would just quickly revert to old processes and hunt down resources used previously, the ones before this new program was implemented. Eventually, they just didn't bother calling for him anymore.

Rose happened to be present at a couple of incidents where a counsellor was frustrated by Boris's inability to help with a client, but when a gathering would move into the manager's office, Boris would sweet-talk a spin of the situation that would deflect attention away from his shortcomings. With the client often unable to speak English well, Boris could alter the understanding of a situation with the manager such that communication issues were minimized.

All this meant that negative feedback regarding Boris didn't often get back to the team supervisor or administrators. Or if it did, Rose noticed that the supervisor would be quick to support Boris or accept his story, as if he didn't want to deal with the mistake that had been made in hiring someone not qualified for the position.

These deceitful activities continued. As the weeks went by, Boris's shenanigans during working hours became a matter of speculation. Like a kind of Sasquatch, hazy rumours would circulate of sightings in malls, banks, or on the street. For instance, one day the two ladies left a community centre meeting only to see Boris bringing in his own child to use one of the programs at the site.

Once, a senior counselor approached our team to provide information and was surprised to see Boris there because he had contacted her earlier only to get information about programs for his own child, not to seek out information for doing his job helping the community to which he had been assigned.

Rose was not one to let such injustices pass. Rose challenged Boris to take professional pride in his work and not let down the Far Eastern community that he was responsible for, but he dismissed her concerns and audaciously suggested that his only interest in the job was in being able to disappear, or, as he put it, "flexibility."

"We are all just here for a buck or two," he would say.

Rose agreed, but re-emphasized that we may as well do the best job we can while we are here. She said that he was occupying the position of someone from that Far Eastern community who could actually help the vulnerable clients he was responsible for, and that his "buck or two" could have come from the previous job he had already held within the same organization. Boris clearly didn't understand her concern, and irritably left the room. Upset with this attitude, she took the next step which was to petition the team supervisor to rein in Boris's abuses, but after a mild reprimand followed by a few full days at his desk, Boris once again vanished from the scene.

The months went by with the two ladies working hard with their respective communities. Eventually, the time came for submitting their reports for the quarter, detailing each client served. For client numbers, Rose had far exceeded the minimum required by the program, and Sophie similarly had no problem meeting her target. To everyone's surprise, Boris also handed in numbers consistent with the size of the Far Eastern community he was servicing. Though he rarely had clients in his office and didn't get calls to attend the various sites, he still presented a full client list in his report. With no sign-in/sign-out sheet, or any other tracking evidence, nothing could be cross-referenced to the data he submitted. Nevertheless, Rose and Sophie understood now why he had lately been so busy pulling files from the filing cabinet.

The months went by in a similar fashion, and the time came again for each team member to submit their report for the second quarter. In a move quite telling, regarding how secure Boris felt in his position, his second report turned out to be identical to the first: name for name, incident for incident, the two reports were exactly the same. Amazingly, he did not even change the dates from those of the last quarter. He hadn't even put in the effort to manufacture second-quarter dates.

Rose could not let such a thing slide. If his report was submitted to headquarters along with those of the other two, the entire team's reputation would be compromised. Beyond that, her moral compass was oriented toward the lack of service that the Far Eastern community was experiencing. Rose talked privately with Boris about his behaviour and the fraudulent nature of the reports he was submitting. She asked that he submit his true numbers and adjust his efforts toward actually helping the community he had been assigned. In a disturbingly abusive and dismissive manner, he brushed her off and walked away.

Shortly afterward, the team was assembled for a records review with the manager to identify service improvement opportunities. This seemed an appropriate venue for Rose to bring up the shoddy data issue, whereupon she witnessed an impressive display by Boris of apologies laced with explanations about being so busy, unfortunate entry errors, database glitches, the same clients all returned, etc. After the meeting, the manager talked to Rose privately and strongly scolded her for bringing up job performance negatives in an open meeting, telling her that, as union workers, problems should first be worked out between peers before going up the management chain. Rose mentioned that she had indeed tried that already and was thanked with abuse while no change in behaviour had occurred.

The manager then talked privately with Boris, but amazingly the following weeks produced no improvement. The team's freeloader continued to keep busy with collecting a paycheck for doing no work.

This inspired Rose to do a little digging about Boris and the manager, and she discovered that they knew each other from a previous working relationship, making it likely that the manager had been aware all along that Boris did not meet the language requirement for this community service position, and had hired him without any regard for consequences to the Far Eastern community. What made it even more galling was that the team's published brochure boldly stated that Boris knew five languages, as if a spectacular lie in this context simply didn't matter since this was only an immigrant program. That management didn't appear to care seemed more and more evident when she remembered the program's introductory meeting where Boris was asked why he applied for this job, and he boldly offered as reasons, "a good retirement and job security". He said nothing in regard to his credentials or his interest in the job itself. He also added as an additional qualification that he used to support this beautiful community in his capacity of repairing people's appliances. A quick diversion by the manger had spared everyone from the need to examine the relevance of that statement. Recalling the incident got Rose to suspecting that the organization had little real interest in this federal attempt to assist immigrants.

By keeping her ear to the ground, she found through office allies that indeed there was real resistance to spending resources on giving special attention to the issues of newcomers. Because the program was mandated federally, the administration had no choice but to implement it, but there seemed to be a generalized yearning to just do things the way they had always been done. This may have been normal bureaucratic laziness, or possibly a darker grumbling about those annoying *ethnics*. Certainly, the tolerance displayed for the deeply substandard work of the white team member charged with servicing the Far Eastern community of the region, told her that managerial sentiment leaned toward the second motivation.

As is her nature, she pursued the matter further, not wanting to let this injustice go unchallenged. Rose wrote an email to the team's manager detailing the problems she felt must be addressed:

- Two of the team members work hard at their jobs, presenting workshops, helping clients with their unique integration issues, and keeping careful records. To see the third team member essentially not working at all is insulting and frustrating.
- Clearly the records of Boris's past two periods were fabricated, even to the point of the second quarter's data being identical, dates and all, to the first quarter's data. Where is the accountability for that?
- Given the explicit mandate and language requirements of the federal government in setting up this program, why was Boris hired when he had no relevant experience and no language skill for the community he was hired to serve?

- How is this working; are we going to take this indecency as far as we can go to ensure there is no service to the Far Eastern community in question? And what term should we use to describe the motivation for that? Racism, perhaps?

Not surprisingly, the manager was unhappy with her boldness of language and her questioning his management of the situation. Once again, he said that she has to resolve the issue at the peer level first. Of course, that had already been done as the manager knew. This time she made it a matter of record by emailing Boris with a similar list of his misdemeanors, as well as accusing him of taking the position he held away from a more qualified person, thus reducing the effectiveness of a program meant to help new Canadians integrate successfully into society.

With the confidence of one who seemed aware that he was immune to scrutiny, Boris did not even bother to respond. So, realizing that her own work was lagging because of her attention to all this, Rose decided to refocus fully on her duties to her community and wait to see what other opportunities might arise to address her grievance. Rose believed that knowing the world was full of irredeemably bad people was no excuse for laying low when encountering wrongdoing, just to protect a pension or avoid disputes. Letting exploiters get away with their actions only encourages them to continue or do worse.

By the end of the first year, Boris's low level of competency and work ethic was generally known in the region. Counselors didn't bother using him as a resource for their Far Eastern clients. Yet no one challenged the situation or came forward to question why only two of the three major immigrant communities were getting first-rate attention from the new program. Perhaps "immigrant" was the key word and nobody judged the effort to be worth it.

Rose was quite upset by this situation because she and her Chinese colleague Sophie, being strongly involved in their communities, knew of the stresses their clients were under and how beneficial were the services they were providing in guiding people to the resources that helped them make their first year or two in Canada easier. They knew that if there was a certain percentage of abused women or suicidal children in their own communities, then those numbers were probably similar in the Far Eastern community that was not being serviced properly. In fact, Rose knew of one young suicide in that community. Who's to know if it could have been prevented if the proper and competent person had been hired as the third team member. Rose began unofficially using people that she knew in that Far East Asian community as contacts for any cases from that community that she ran across, but she was busy with her own work and there wasn't much she could do.

With most sites realizing that Boris was not an effective resource for them, Rose was able to recruit a couple of counselors who supported her in another communication to management. Front-line workers wanted to know why there were two hard-working and effective, though under-appreciated, members of this new program, but also one so obviously unproductive member. They pointed out how much good work could be done if everyone on the team was equally conscientious. The question was asked if management had no standards of fairness to guide them in running their show, or was protection of incompetence what a unionized workplace meant.

Again, no attention seemed to be paid to the real problem, and if they were dealing with him behind scenes, it did not seem to have any effect; he was still there to do as he pleased. Management instead chose to spend their energies reprimanding Rose and telling her not to mind the business of other employees.

Since that level of management seemed not to understand that such minding of employees was indeed *their* job, she went to higher management to see what sort of bureaucratic nonsense they might have to offer as an excuse for doing nothing about fraud, incompetence and lying. Unsurprisingly, they told her that they were not mandated to "micro-manage" front-line workers.

So now it was the union's turn to help solve the problem if they chose to. However, when Rose went to her representative, she was given the same advice about ignoring anything a co-worker does and leaving everything up to management's discretion, not only regarding whether to respond to the problem, but even whether they chose to perceive it. In fact, the content of the discussion and the tone of reprimand from the union rep were so in line with management's phrasing of the matter, that it seemed as if the two had colluded. When she presented that challenge, the rep was not happy, but consented to look at the falsified records. She could not help but see that the allegations were true, but she simply agreed to that and then told Rose to leave.

With all these experiences, Rose came to realize that nothing was going to be done about the situation. She actually gave serious consideration to resigning. The integrity of the program was compromised, and she wondered if it was worth working for, and with, people that seemed to care very little about the goals and outcomes that she herself considered valuable.

It appeared that the managers considered the program to be an imposition, and they also had no interest in Rose's attempts to make it the best it could be. To her, it seemed those two elements could be explained by racism and sexism. Racism, because the program was specifically designed to serve immigrants and help them integrate into Canadian society, and a white staff member, with no knowledge of, or connection to, the Far East Asian community he was responsible for, was allowed to completely ignore it. And sexism, because the male team member that was perpetrating the wrongdoing, who was hired through an old boy's network that he continued to nurture, was feeling no repercussions for his conduct, while a woman challenging that state of affairs was the one being reprimanded.

In the end, Rose decided to stay because she knew that the work she was doing was important to the community of new Canadians that she now felt a strong measure of responsibility for.

So, she did her best to focus on her job and let her ethical duty rest for the time being, until perhaps another opportunity arose. Year after year she carried on, gaining strength from the significant help she was able to give to so many people, but also enduring the proximity of such unprincipled behaviour by Boris and the team's management. If a healthy work environment depends on colleagues and supervisors being engaged with an organization's mission and supporting the avowed goals of the team, then the lack of such backing meant that Rose had to deal with more than she should.

Eventually, the administration was able to get the annoying program shut down and out of their hair. Although the entire federal program was phased out a year later, the organization eagerly shut their local branch down early, quite likely so that one more year was not available for a scandal to break out if the fraud and incompetence within their team were to escape into some kind of scandalous media disaster.

It really is impressive that heavily multicultural countries such as Australia, Canada and the United States have many programs in place that have been developed by governments for the purpose of helping the disenfranchised and others in need, whether they are citizens of many generations or the newest of immigrants. It is unfortunate that Rose felt that she could not trust those programs anymore. Are the same things going on behind the scenes elsewhere? In all programs? Some of them? Just a few?

What we do in a day is important. We carry out our responsibilities as best we can and expect that everyone around us will do the same, so that we can all build a better world day by day. If we encounter injustices, we can ignore them or sweep them under the rug, but it will be a lesser world as a result, with more abuses in society and an increase of cynicism in individuals. We cannot let the great consumerist fear of losing a job or a pension prevent us from instinctively challenging wrongdoing as it occurs. And if confronting the situation by going through "proper" management channels results in no correction of the misconduct, the life

of a whistleblower can be difficult indeed, not only because of the inevitable bureaucratic pushback, but because the whistleblower, usually being a person with a higher than average ethical sense, must continue to witness the crimes she or he is defying. We must oppose the rigid and inflexible bureaucracy model that always seems to resist the encouragement of our better instincts and philosophies.

In the end, management and the union shuffled Boris into his previous position, the very one that he had run away from because of the restrictive hours he hated so much. They also offered a position to Rose, but her pride didn't allow her to accept staying with an organization that had treated her and the situation as poorly and disgracefully as it had. So, she moved on to a new chapter in her life, her third career in as many years. This one seems to be working out well for her.

Nadiya: – Russian; Hope. – Arabic; Tender, delicate. – Swahili; Caller

Klaus: Danish; Victory of the People

Anastasia: Slavic; Resurrection

Bolodenko: Slavic; Peaceful

Akilah: Arabic; Clever, bright

PEOPLE

It is that time of the year again. The mall is furiously busy, especially in the evening. Inside, the air is thick with the heat and exhalations of thousands of people. How many have the flu, pushing through their nauseous haze to fulfil their Yuletide duties?

She is trying to use her break to complete her final assignment for the term, but is distracted by all the people passing to and fro, scouring clothing boutiques for just the right item, catching a meal in the food court, then diving back into the fray for the next item on their lists.

She tries again to focus on her studies as the people feverishly shop, buying presents, interesting and dull, for all the people they adore and despise, fulfilling the Christmas law. There has to be a tree and lots of presents under it, a tradition followed by many around the globe.

Her break is over, so she packs up her things and walks back to the store where she works.

"Ah, I did not complete this chapter," she mumbles as she heads to the back of the store to put away her bag. "But how could I, with all those smells and all the bustling activity around this time of year."

Her friend greets her, "Did you have a good break, Nadiya?"

"Ah, it was okay. I rested somewhat and had my break, but I couldn't finish my chapter for the last assignment."

"Well look, I'm done with my semester, so how about you leave early and I will cover for you."

"Oh, thanks Klaus, you dear one, but I need the money. I have to help my mom buy what she needs for my sister. When do you graduate, by the way?"

"This is my last year. I'll be done by spring."

"So, then you will leave us soon?"

"Well, if I can find a good job, yes, I will leave, but there are not many out there. I'm making decent money now as the manager of two stores. I've been working here since high school, so I'm doing alright for the time being. Even with my bachelor's degree this spring, I know I cannot have a better paying job than this one, so I'm aiming for a Master's in Sociology."

"Good for you, Klaus. You know, I'm sure I will have to do the same. We live in a relatively small city, and with so many colleges and universities pushing out graduates each year, how can we all get employment related to our fields of study? I feel it's becoming worse every year. It's alarming."

"It sure is!" says Klaus as he folds clothes scattered about by customers. "Look, I meant it. Go home a couple of hours early. Hey, I am the manager. I won't take it off your paycheck. I know how much you need it."

Nadiya looks at him appreciatively, "You are so sweet. I know you did the same last week for Samuel, working two extra hours covering for him and still paying his full wages."

"How do you know? He wasn't supposed to share this information. If management finds out, I am in trouble!"

"Don't worry, we don't talk about it, because we too would be in trouble."

"I only do this for you and Samuel, as you two are so hard-working and smart. I want you both to complete your education and get to working in your field." He pauses and winks at her, "By the way, are you and Samuel going out? I mean, are you a couple? You spend a lot of time together."

"No, you silly! Samuel is gay and I'm his best friend, so we talk a lot and he tells me of his troubles." Klaus stops working to look at her for a bit as she opens the boxes of new arrivals and gives them to Klaus for sorting. "Oh, I did not know that - hmm. He is a nice young man, and I really like him. I've seen you two chit-chatting a lot and spending lunch or breaks together. Sorry for being nosy. What are his troubles? If you can tell me, of course."

"Ah ... yes, I guess I can tell you, since in a way you probably know his problems as being the general ones all gay people face. You know, the usual unfair treatment they suffer from ignorant people; even those within their own families."

"I do know; what a shame! You would think by now, with so much more awareness in schools and workplaces, that most people would just stop making a big deal of it." He sighs as he continues working.

Nadiya goes to attend to a customer. *"Silly me,"* Klaus thinks, watching her walk away. *"I thought they were an item. I had better ask her out before it's too late."* He smiles while working, from time to time looking at Nadiya as she deals with customers.

Hours pass and closing time arrives. Klaus has let everyone go, and is making the shelves presentable for the following day. He finally closes up, and as he is locking the door, he glances over to the main entrance and sees Nadiya's mother outside struggling toward the doors, pale and breathless with the heavy bags she is carrying. He runs to open the door for her, "Hey, hey, dear lady, let me help you!"

"Oh, hi Klaus. Thanks! Yes, they are rather heavy."

"What are they, groceries?"

"Yes, plus this-and-that for the kids. Did Nadiya go home already? I thought she was closing the store tonight."

"Well, she was worried about her last assignment, so I let her go home early."

"Oh, that's so kind of you, thanks. Yes, she was worried this morning, thinking there is no way she would be able to complete the last assignment tonight. When did she leave?"

"I let her go a few hours ago, and I'm sure by the time you get home you'll find her happy that she has everything done."

They walk out of the mall together. She reaches for the bags Klaus is holding so she can go to her bus stop. "Don't even think about it," Klaus says as he continues walking. "I will drive you. You're on my way anyway."

The tired woman doesn't protest and happily limps after him toward his car.

He drops her bags off at the front door and wishes her a happy evening with her kids, then drives away. As she opens the door Nadiya comes out of the living room along with her brother to help her with the bags.

"You're home a bit early," says Nadiya. "Did you get a ride home?"

"Ah, it was your kind boss, Klaus. I went to meet you at the store and he told me I was on his way home."

Nadiya doesn't respond, thinking, *"He lives totally in the opposite direction. Hmm, maybe he was going somewhere else."* They begin unpacking the bags and putting the groceries away.

"Did you complete your assignment, darling?"

"Yes mother, I did; and I did well, I think. I'm happy with it."

"Great, what did you eat for dinner, and how about Anastasia? Did you make sure she had dinner? Did she do her homework? She is on that damn cell phone all the time."

"Yes mother, don't worry. Go take a shower and go to bed, you look exhausted."

Mother gives her a hug and a kiss then heads down the hallway. Nadiya and her brother watch her as she disappears into the bathroom. They look at each other remorsefully, and in frustration Nadiya bangs the chair she's been leaning on. "She shouldn't work anymore. She has been working since we arrived in this country, as well as all her life back home since she was a teenager. We should make her sit at home and relax for the rest of her life."

"I couldn't agree more," says Bolodenko. "She has done enough for us. Maybe we should send her on a vacation to a nice warm place."

"Vacation? Do we have the money for that? I like the idea though."

"Well, I just signed a contract!" says Bolodenko with a big grin on his face.

"Oh, get out of here! Are you serious?"

"I am! It was about time. I graduated two years ago and I've been sending résumés out ever since. Though it's not a hundred percent my field, it pays much better than the odd jobs I've been doing so far. One step at a time! I begin in the new year, so I'm hoping I can send her on a good trip in the spring. What do you say?"

"I say it's a great idea, but I hope you include Anastasia in the trip. Mother won't go anywhere without her, and to be honest it's better that they are together. That little girl is becoming a young lady. She needs some fun too. I'll help!"

"No, no, I'll take care of it. You're right, mother won't go without her. Also, every year Anastasia's friends show off about their spring break vacations and she just has to sigh and smile; she never complains. We'll tell her it's her pre-graduation gift."

"Ah yes, I forgot that our little sister is graduating from high school this year."

They continue cleaning and doing their best so that when their mother comes out of the shower there is nothing for her to do, and she can go right to bed. They even prepare all the lunches for the next day. As they work away around their little apartment, mother comes out to sit in the living room drying her hair with towels. Nadiya brings her tea and some sweets while her son sits on the other side of the sofa and gives his mother a foot rub. She sighs and looks at her children fondly.

"So, how was your day, my darling Bolodenko?"

"Fine mother, and actually I have some good news."

"Oh, what is it?"

"Okay, but please let me finish everything I have to say. You are not to argue with me." Mother gives her son a puzzled look, not understanding what is going on.

"Well, I signed a contract today, and I now have a much better job with much more pay. So, I want you to hand in your resignation, and as of this March you are not going to work anymore. You have done enough; please stay home as of this March. Also, I am planning a vacation for you and Anastasia. You take your vacation, and when you return, she will go back to school and you can do whatever you like. Take some courses, maybe do some painting, take up ballroom dancing; whatever you like. No work for you anymore, young lady. Just bringing us here from that war-torn area was a monumental task, yet it didn't end there. You worked so hard helping us through school and doing anything else you could for us. So now it's our time. You rest, we provide!"

Nadiya looks at her brother with deep affection, then holds her mother's hand and kisses it. "He's right, mother! It's about time for you to retire."

"What are you two talking about? I am not even sixty yet. I still have a few good years before I retire. And don't forget, if I resign now I cannot have my pension."

"Sure, you can!" says Bolodenko. "When you turn sixty-five you can start receiving your government pension, plus the retirement savings you have put aside from your past twenty years of employment. And with our help, there will be plenty."

Mother regards her children proudly. "Look, it would be so boring to stop working now." She shifts herself into a more comfortable position. "Although I am feeling quite worn out right now, and I do tire of the long hours. I really don't want to retire right now, but I suppose I could work part time; at least until I'm sixty." She smiles at them, "I suppose you two have a point. I guess I would like to take up ballroom dancing if I just worked part time. Ah, my sweet darlings!" She sits up and holds them both.

"What do you say Nadiya, should we let her work part time?"

"Well, yes, we can see how she does. Okay mother, you are allowed to work part time up to your sixties." They laugh at this scene of the mother taking orders from her children. They joke and banter for a while longer, then retire to their rooms to turn in for the night.

❖ ❖ ❖

"What a sunny and beautiful day! The weather forecast said it would be raining," says Nadiya.

Samuel looks out and smiles, "Glad they made that mistake. Yes, it certainly is gorgeous today; and how bright it is! I love it!"

They continue complimenting the day as they walk away from the school to begin their Christmas holiday. They thank each other for the gifts they exchanged earlier, hug, then go their separate ways. Nadiya looks at her watch, *"Oops, I'll be late for my meeting with Klaus; hopefully he'll do what I said and wait in the store for me to arrive, then take his break."*

She rushes to catch her bus, finds a seat, and throws her exhausted body onto it. Gazing out the window, enjoying the pleasant sun, it doesn't take long before she falls asleep in her seat.

"Hello, hey, hey, get up! It's the end of the line." The bus driver shakes her awake. Nadiya opens her eyes and looks around, "Where am I?"

"You are in my bus, darling. You must be very tired to sleep through that loudspeaker announcing each stop."

"What? Then I have passed my stop! Ah, I'll be late! I have to go back! I'm going to work! We were to have a meeting! Ah, he'll be late for his next job!" She continues rambling as she tries to get off the bus.

"Sit down, young lady," says the driver kindly with her hand on Nadiya's shoulder. "Don't worry, I'm heading back again in a few minutes. Sit and wait and I will take you back."

Nadiya looks at the driver with appreciation, thanks her, and takes out her phone.

"Good idea, call your work and tell them how tired you were, and that you passed out." She winks and goes back to the front to check in with dispatch.

Nadiya calls her work and, close to tears, explains what happened; but clearly there is no stress coming from the other end of the line, as she is soon smiling at the situation.

As soon as she gets to work, Klaus welcomes her with a big smile, "How was your nap, sleepy head?"

Her other co-workers laugh and welcome her. Samuel says, "Ah, there you are. I didn't know you were working today."

"I'm not. What are you doing here?"

"Klaus asked me to come in to cover for him because he is having lunch with a friend. Um, that's you?"

"Yes, I have a meeting with Klaus. He said he needs to talk to me and..."

Klaus is at the door and ready to go. "You two can chit-chat later," he says, "I'm taking this young lady out for lunch."

Nadiya and Samuel exchange a look and a smile as Klaus gently pulls Nadiya's arm. "Let's go."

"What's the occasion? You said you needed to talk to me and I thought it was about work. I didn't know we were going for lunch. I could have gone home to change and meet up with you later."

"What? No, no worries! It's not like I haven't seen you at your worst as well as your best. After all, you just fell asleep on a bus!" They laugh about it as she recalls the scene and talks about the kind bus driver.

Holding her arm he guides her toward the mall entrance.

"Oh, we're not eating here?"

"No. I am taking you to your favourite restaurant."

"But why? My birthday isn't until next month. Are you talking about the place we went with our co-workers last year on my birthday?"

"Yes, and you liked it so much that I thought I would take you there now."

"Oh, then I definitely should go home and change. I'm in my casuals. I didn't even have a shower this morning; all I was doing was writing an exam. What is going on?"

Klaus laughs cheerfully, telling her not to worry about it. They walk to the restaurant across from the mall and he opens the door for her. The waiter welcomes them. Klaus says, "I have a reservation. I asked for the corner table facing the mountains."

"Oh yes, it's all set sir; please follow me." He guides them to their table, a beautiful setting in the corner at the large window facing the mountain range in the distance. There is a bouquet of roses in a beautiful vase on the table and Nadiya laughs nervously. "They put flowers on the table too? I've never seen that before."

"I asked them to. They are yours to take with you when we leave." He holds her chair while she sits, then takes his own seat.

"Okay, what is this? What's going on? What are you doing, Klaus?"

"Are you angry with me before even hearing me?"

"I'm sorry Klaus, I thought you wanted to talk about work like we do sometimes; but in this expensive restaurant? With a reservation? And roses? I have a right to be alarmed and ask questions, don't I?"

"Look, how long have we known each other? Four, close to five years?" Nadiya wants to say something, but with a soft gesture and a kind gaze he invites her to wait and just listen.

He looks at the floor, then into her eyes and says, "We know each other to be honest and hard-working people, and we regularly help each other, and others too, in any way we can. We clearly have mutual respect for one another." He pauses for a bit, and then looks into her eyes tenderly, "I do not need to gain your trust; I know I already have it. So, I thought I could take you to lunch in this beautiful setting and ask if you would go out with me; you know, so that we can get to know one another in a romantic way. I have strong feelings for you, and I have wanted to ask you out for a while now, but I thought you and Samuel were an item, so I respected you both and didn't say anything. Then you said you were only friends. I didn't want to lose you to David, because I know he likes you and he may ask you out any day."

"Well, he could ask," Nadiya says with a sour look, "but my answer would definitely be no. I do not like him, not even as a co-worker. He's lazy and has no respect for women. He thinks that because of his looks everybody melts for him. No sir, not me! I want a partner; someone who is considerate, and is co-operative and supportive; someone who has a goal and a plan, including getting a good education. Above all, he has to be respectful to all women, and David doesn't even respect his own mother."

"Well great then, it appears I needn't worry about him. Anyone else around that I should know about?" He smiles and winks at her and continues, "Now I know you don't have a boyfriend, but I also don't know if you like me the way I like you."

They look at each other quietly for a few long seconds, then she smiles, showing off the beautiful dimples in her pretty cheeks. She winks at him saying, "I thought you would never ask. I've been waiting long enough!"

Klaus chuckles and looks at her happily. He takes her hand and shakes his head, "Then my friends are right when they say I have no clue about women. So you liked me too, hey? Whew, I was a bit nervous, let me tell you. I'm so glad we're on the right path."

Nadiya smiles and relaxes, settling in to enjoy the lunch. They order their meals, joking and laughing as they enjoy their food and wine, and talk about various things. At one point, Nadiya thanks him for driving her mother home the night before.

"Oh, of course, I was happy to! The poor woman was so tired. I actually like your mother very much."

"Well, she really is a wonderful woman. She's my mother and naturally I love her for that, but I also like her for the person she is. Did I ever tell you she was an engineer back home?"

"No, you didn't. What is she doing working in retail here?"

"Well, we came here over twenty years ago. I think I was three years old and my brother was in grade two. My sister was born here. My parents were both professionals; however, they didn't have Canadian degrees or experience, so they could never work in their field. My father went up north to work in a mine, hoping to make his way up to his former position as a mining engineer, but he was never allowed to progress very far. Instead he died of lung cancer when my sister was only two years old. Since then my mother has worked hard to keep the family together."

Klaus holds her hand and puts his forehead on hers, "I am so sorry, my dear. I did not know that."

"Thank you, Klaus. Actually, last night my brother and I decided to send our mother on a vacation, and we also asked her not to work anymore. She didn't accept that, but agreed to reduce her hours to part time, which is good enough for now. What about your parents; what are they doing? We have never talked about our families before."

"How sweet of you two to help your mother. I wish I could have done something like that for my mother. She worked so hard too, and died so young. It was not her time; she wasn't even forty yet."

"Oh, don't say that! Ah, I didn't know you lost your mother. I regret asking."

"No, no, I'm glad you did. It's good to talk about her with someone. I have missed her. On lonely days I think about her a lot. She was a beautiful woman with the kindest heart. I was the only child, and my parents adored one another. They had a great relationship. When my mother became ill, my father took care of her for a long time. When treatments didn't work and she finally passed away after all that suffering, my father became severely depressed and I had to take care of him for a while. Eventually he put himself together when he noticed my marks at school falling behind. He also noticed I had lost weight and I didn't look all that well. It was as if my appearance woke him out of a stupor, and he seemed to shake off his mournful life. I once more saw the wonderful father he had always been. He went back to work, and cooked and cleaned around the home again and made sure I got back on track with my schooling. He never married again, saying, 'There is no woman out there to love and understand me like your mother did.' He thinks it's fine to be just the two of us."

Nadiya looks at him intensely, listening to his story and seeing the high respect he has for his mother and who she was. "It seems we both had our share of unfairness in this world. Well, here we are now. I can say I always liked your intelligence, but I also admired your respect for women. I never saw you flirt with the girls at work or at company parties; unlike that insolent David. He flirts with everyone! Boy, I do not like him!"

"Well, I'm so sorry that I thought you did, and I'm happy that I finally asked you out."

"I never saw you with any girl, come to think of it. Didn't you ever have a girlfriend?"

"Sure, I had two. One was in high school and we were together from grade ten to graduation. But then she was accepted at the University of Toronto and went east. Later, I met a young passionate Palestinian girl at my university here, and we fell in love and planned to get married."

At this point Klaus is quiet and looks down so Nadiya won't see his tears, but she notices and softly caresses his hands, "Tell me what happened; tell me!"

"Perhaps you have heard about the Palestinians, and their decades-long problems with Israel."

"Yes, they are fighting for two separate states, right? But when were they one state that now they want to separate? I'm a bit unclear with that part."

"Ah my dear, I guess they have had petty wars on and off going back to their civil war of 1948, shortly after the Second World War. It may even go further back, but I have been reading about the region's recent history. I began following events seriously right after I met Akilah. Hey, I wanted to impress her, so I had to get up to speed."

Nadiya slaps the back of his hand softly and says, "You couldn't impress her with a favourite restaurant and a bunch of roses?"

They both laugh. After a short pause Klaus holds her hand, looks into her eyes, and says, "It was different then. I didn't know her culture and I was afraid to lose her. Anyway, where was I? Ah yes; you see, before the war Jews lived everywhere as they do now, but they never had a country of their own. They were scattered around the world, though they were often separated from the mainstream population in particular countries. Well, after World War II the Western world helped them establish their own country, called Israel, in the area northeast of Egypt known then as Palestine. Of course, there were already people living there, so the wars began from then to today. At first it was about liberating Jews from the discrimination and persecution that they had been experiencing during their diaspora, but now it seems to be different. Today's hostile Israeli government doesn't want to share the land with those original inhabitants. They keep making new settlements in every corner of Palestine, pushing away the inhabitants; they've been doing it since 1948. Now "Palestine" seems to refer only to the non-Israeli part of that land, and Akilah was part of an organization that was gathering aid for Palestinians. I got involved and began helping too. Have you heard about the difficult life Palestinians have?"

"Yes, I heard about that, but not in much detail."

"In many places they have limited work, sub-standard shelter, and lack of healthcare, food and many other things. We wanted to help. Together we joined one group assembling an expedition to deliver aid. We gathered medicine, food, clothing and other supplies. The plan was to sail it all over to Palestine in a ship. It was a long and difficult journey, but we made it. However, when we arrived, the Israeli navy was there preventing us from passing through. They started searching the ship and were very disrespectful to Arabs or others who looked like the locals. They even hit them any chance they got.”

“Did they hit you too?”

“No, I seemed to get less *special attention* as a white man. Nonetheless, they were very rude to everyone on board because we were challenging their agenda of occupation, blockades, and settlement construction on Palestinian land. So no, they were not very accommodating to any of us. Anyway, that trip was the most educational event of my life, eye and mind opening. Akilah tried to reason with them, assuring them that we were only attempting to get basic necessities of life to people.”

“What a brave girl.”

“Well, nothing worked. They ordered us to turn around and leave and told us to never come back. A few members of our group went with the authorities to the city to pursue more negotiations. While they were away Akilah formulated a crazy plan. She filled two big backpacks with materials and said she was going to take one of the ship's small boats at night to deliver them. Of course, I wouldn't let her go alone, so the two of us loaded the boat and set off across the dark, choppy sea toward the city. We arrived on shore, thrilled about our little adventure, and began emptying the boat. But before we could start trekking inland, soldiers emerged from the dark night to surround us. They arrested both of us and took us to their station where, for the last time, I saw the frightened face and tearful, beautiful eyes of Akilah."

Nadiya listens breathlessly, staring at Klaus, impatiently waiting for him to continue.

After a minute, Klaus raises his eyes, "I called my father right away to tell him what had happened, and I had him contact Akilah's family. Our fathers arrived two days later. I was released once I had signed a document agreeing that I would never enter Israel again. However, they kept Akilah and then arrested her father too. I had to leave, but my father stayed to demand answers as to why they had arrested a Canadian citizen who was there simply to ask for his daughter. He could get nowhere with the local authorities, so my father went to our embassy in Tel Aviv and demanded the release of the father and daughter. I waited in Damascus for them to join me. After a couple of stressful weeks, they finally met me there."

Klaus takes a deep breath and exhales it slowly. "I went to the airport to see her as soon as she arrived. I cannot describe the anxious state of my mind as they emerged from the plane. In just two weeks, both men had noticeably lost weight, in particular Akilah's father. I looked behind them, but I could not see Akilah. My father held me and said he was sorry. I looked at her father, and his tearful eyes looked straight into mine, 'They killed her.'"

Tears run down Klaus's face, "I was dumbfounded, and couldn't even speak to ask them what had happened. Apparently, they told her father that she was shot while trying to escape. I was out of my mind, trashing everything in my way and I ran outside. The two fathers chased me down and tried to comfort me, and eventually I pulled myself together. Her body was already on its way to Canada, so we headed home for the funeral."

Klaus looks down as he lets Nadiya caress his hands. She can't think what to say, so they sit quietly together for some time.

Eventually Klaus looks up into her tearful eyes and apologizes for upsetting her, "I should only have said that I did have a girlfriend, we wanted to get married, but something happened and she passed away. I shouldn't have made you so upset on our first date. I'm so sorry."

"Do not apologize for the crimes of others. For sure I am sad, but that passionate young girl was killed for her beliefs and for trying to help others; and you're worried if I'm upset? Look, I know where you're coming from. People don't like to hear distressing stories or get involved in the troubles of others, because then they would be forced to care about what happens to them. But don't think that I'm one of those pampered people or that…"

But before she can say anymore, Klaus takes her hands and kisses them, then stands to lean over the table and kiss her forehead, "I definitely did not mean it that way. I would have told you the story eventually; I just meant I perhaps shouldn't really talk about it on our first date."

"Ah, pish posh, it doesn't matter. I would be…" Nadiya can't finish her sentence as tears begin to run down her cheeks. Her voice breaking, she says, "I cannot believe what a cruel world we are living in, and how the lives of so many people mean so little. All kinds of wars and conflicts wreaking havoc in and around resource-rich or strategic regions of our world, and we here in the developed world can only think about keeping busy with shopping, entertainment, and vacations in hot-spot resorts. We don't even want to hear about anything else. What is it with us? When did we become so selfish?"

Klaus tries to calm her down but she resists, and is not happy that he even attempts to stop her. She continues, "You know yesterday at work, I heard a couple of people complaining about the tsunami of refugees moving around Europe, and even whining about some of them coming here. I just wanted to jump in and challenge them; ask them if they thought those people should stay in the war zones to die, just so they don't mess up your perfect little life. I wanted to question what they would do in the same situation; stay or flee to a safer place? Rrrr, it's so frustrating! I don't know what to say Klaus, how can we stop all these wars?"

Nadiya cleans away her tears and looks into Klaus's worried eyes, then says, "Oh, your story really is so heartbreaking; when did this happen?"

"About twelve years ago. Yes, it was during one of those intifadas that accomplishes not much more than an escalation of economic ruin, blockades, and attacks on Palestinians. Dozens of Israelis die and hundreds, if not thousands, of Palestinians die. When everything calms down, Israel gets back to the business of taking more land and creating more settlements. This has been going on since 1948, while the world sits back and watches. So there you have it; I became involved in trying to do something about the situation, and all I did was help my lovely fiancée to her death. It took me a few years to come to terms with it and to be able to forgive myself. I put the blame on me for letting her get into that boat and go on that crazy mission. I thought I should never be allowed to love again. Then you came along."

"But you were so cold when we first met. You didn't seem to like me back then, did you?"

"Oh no, it wasn't like that. I was aloof with everyone, not only you. I had to work and complete my schooling and, as my father put it, 'Come back to the land of the living.' I did not like life's cruelties. I didn't like the shallow culture around me; so I stayed away from everyone. Just went to school and worked."

With one hand Klaus tops up the wine in each glass, and with the other holds Nadiya's hand, "We've been working together daily for a while now. Over that much time we naturally learn about one another. As time passed I grew fond of your integrity and kindness, and above all I fell for those beautiful dimples on your cheeks."

Nadiya laughs and cries at the same time, "Do you still think about her?"

"Of course; she was the love of my life. We were together for over four years. We dropped out of university and went on aid missions together - actually a few times. Well, it all ended tragically, but that's all over now and life goes on. I cannot live alone forever, and if you don't get angry at me for saying this ..." He pauses a bit and softly says, "I love you Nadiya. I wouldn't ask you out if I didn't. I am not in my twenties anymore, and I am looking for a serious relationship. Akilah and I were supposed to get married after that trip. Over ten years have passed, and I have suffered enough; even her father encourages me to go on with my life. So, as my feelings for you grew, I did not suppress them. I wanted to love you, and hoped you would reciprocate someday."

Nadiya is surprised, as she did not think she would hear about love on her surprise date. She doesn't know what to say, but after briefly gazing at the mountains she says, "I do like you very much Klaus, and I'm feeling that I too would like to begin something serious; because, as you said, I too have come to know you and appreciate every aspect of your personality."

She pauses briefly, and then with the sweetest smile she says, "It's not difficult to fall in love with you, you know."

She looks down and begins playing with her napkin. Klaus is happy. He looks at her with admiration, sure in his heart that she is the one for him, hoping she feels that way too; if not today, then sometime soon. They sip their wine and fall into light chit-chat about work and the weather. They joke about the approach of Valentine's Day, the next step in the retail cycle following Christmas, when businesses begin to encourage people to remember their partners just for one day, so that they can keep the cash registers ringing.

Soon their talk becomes serious again as they discuss the chaotic state of the planet; wars, poverty and intolerances, and the need to gather peace-loving people together in the fight for a more co-operative and equitable world. They give vent to their disappointments at the unending torments and displacements of so many millions as whole cities and societies are destroyed.

They discuss the need for heightened awareness across the world so that everyone can see what is really going on with the greedy fight for resources, and the true reasons for all the—discord and strife. They feel disheartened knowing that speaking to others about these things will only fall on deaf ears, and that myriad entertainments will keep people of all walks of life too busy to perceive the dark purpose of the mammoth global economic system that their governments maintain to control people and resources.

Eventually they decide to go for a walk. Klaus has the waiter wrap up the flowers for her, then he helps her with her jacket. They walk out into the crowded streets.

"You know Klaus, this time of year bothers me the most. Look how everyone is running around for the best sales, and all I can think about are the people who don't have a proper family or the money to compete in this madness."

"I hear you, and I feel the same. My parents did not have much family here because they were all back in Austria. You know, my mother would have loved you. She too always said the Christmas holidays didn't have the spirit we remembered from years ago. It has become so commercialized."

He reaches for her hand, and Nadiya takes his with a smile. They walk to his car where he asks if she would like a drive around the ocean or maybe a walk by the river. She nods happily, "Both. Let's drive to the river and walk along the dike to the ocean."

"As you wish, my darling." He opens the door for her, then runs around to his side. In the car they fall into discussion about the issue of willful blindness to crimes of the past, ostensibly as a way to move forward and move on, presumably to a bright future of no villains or victims. "A nice thought," says Nadiya, "but that's no justice for those who have suffered outrages, or lost land and loved ones. We can't make it easy for those who have perpetrated crimes, especially if they are ongoing to this day. If we forget, we may be doomed to repeat, and perhaps commit even worse crimes."

"Yes, and that will just bring more chaos," says Klaus.

They drive around a bend in the road and see the beautiful, mighty Fraser River spread out before them. "Ah, what a beautiful day! Not too cold and so sunny!" says Nadiya.

"Yes, a perfect day for us on our first date." They park the car and begin their walk hand-in-hand along the river toward the gorgeous Georgia Strait with the view of distant Vancouver Island. They walk and laugh, almost dancing as light as air with their hands and body gestures, as they disappear around a bend to begin a bright new journey together.

❦ ❦ ❦

Days and nights pass with the unfailing regularity of time; weeks and months go by and a new year begins again as the river of life moves steadily forward, softly or vigorously, bringing Nadiya and Klaus on new adventures at every turn. They grow together as two devoted friends and passionate lovers. By now their family has expanded in different directions. Klaus's father and Nadiya's mother have joined their lonely lives together, and they now live as a happy couple. Anastasia lives with them while she attends university, "Someone has to keep an eye on those two old lovers. They are so distracted with each other that they keep leaving the stove on!"

Klaus and Nadiya have joined a peace organization and are working hard as humanitarian aid workers, always seeking to challenge any callous government that has fallen into the tyranny of enslaving their own people and resources to the corporations and neo-colonial nations that help them stay in power to live like kings. And whenever they return back home to those over-reaching and wealthy lands, the two of them never rest in their mission to break people away from their diversions and ask themselves why it is that, at this peak of humanity's scientific, social and technological advances, there continue to be so many wars with no apparent ability to stop them. How we are all contributing to conditions around the world that generate streams of refugees – millions of people who have no desire to leave their homelands or the memories they cherish – who would merely wish to be left in peace if only the powerbrokers of greed could see social justice as more than just a word to be ignored and an idea to be swept aside?

I would end my short tales with a quote from Romain Rolland, French author (1866 – 1944):

"You desire a popular art? Begin by having a 'People' whose minds are liberated, a people not crushed by misery and continual labour, not brutalized by every superstition and every fanaticism, a people of itself, and victor in the fight that is being waged today."

❖ ❖ ❖

Decades have passed since our two vicious World Wars, yet much discord still rages all around us, stunning proof of our moral and ethical weakness. Hostilities only bring about the decay of civilization. Wars that have been fashioned for profit only create rage among nations. Never-ending wars develop a sense of their normalcy, causing people to become more and more indifferent, preventing the growth of a moral regard for others. With anxieties all around us, we never embark on the work of building the bridges and bonds between peoples the world over, a work that would empower us in bringing enmities and rivalries to an end.

ACKNOWLEDGMENT

To the ones who share humanity's home with all. To those who work tirelessly to bring justice to those with no voice, and improve the lives of the oppressed.

To my dear Murray, my comfort and the wall behind me, who believes in me.

To my dear Jean, who never doubted me; who always offers her lovely smile with deep support.

AUTHOR BIOGRAPHY

Nasreen Pejvack is a published author, with her novel "Amity" published by Inanna Publications, York University Press in October of 2015. Soon after, it was shortlisted for BC's 2016 Ethel Wilson Book Prize.

She left Iran a few years after the 1979 revolution. She lived in Athens for several months, and then left Greece for

 Canada to begin a new life in a peaceful environment. In Ottawa she studied computer programming at Algonquin College and worked in the field for over 11 years (Programmer, Application Developer). She then moved to California to work as a Systems Analyst Project Manager for CNet during the tech boom of the 1990s.

After several years she returned to her new homeland of Canada and BC, where she left the IT field and decided to start a new chapter in her life, studying and working as a counselor and educator, while pursuing a degree in Psychology.

Following her successful novel Amity, she is now here presenting short tales inspired by her experiences of life in Canada.

Her book of poetry "Waiting" was published at the same time as her collection of short tales "Paradise of Downcast," both published in 2018.

Nasreen's other hobby is the research, design, development and presentation of a variety of workshops on various aspects of our society.

Nasreen was a judge for the 2018 BC Ethel Wilson Fiction Prize. Also she is President of Royal City Literary Arts Society since May 2016.